COME LIVE WITH ME

by

Marie Cross

Martin Publishing
35 Exeter Close
TONBRIDGE, Kent
Tel: 01732 350670

ISBN   978 0 9546146 1 5

Cover design Jean Hill
Printed and bound by CPI Antony Rowe, Chippenham and
Eastbourne

CHAPTER 1

Ian was late again. Lucy served the meal, but kept it warm for half an hour before eating hers. Perhaps his train was delayed; maybe there had been an accident? She turned on the TV, but nothing was reported. Surely he hadn't been asked to work another evening – but he'd never been as late as this.

Lucy fetched her law book to study, but the same paragraph floated across her eyes. Finally she closed it with a snap and went to the window to check once again.

It was nearly ten when she heard Ian's key in the lock.

'Lucy, it's me.' His bag thumped on the hall floor.

She rushed out to meet him. 'Where've you been? Why didn't you ring? I've been worried sick. I nearly rang your mother in case you'd gone there, but I didn't want to upset her if you weren't.' Lucy was close to tears with relief.

'I met a friend and we went for a drink.' Ian put his hands in his pockets and jingled his money. 'Down Villiers Street, by Charing Cross Station,' he expanded as he followed her into the kitchen. 'You know the one, we've been there together.'

'Did that take three hours?' she said, her anxiety moving to anger.

'I forgot the time.'

Lucy put his dinner in the microwave and turned the dial. 'You could have phoned.'

'I just forgot, that's all.' Ian sat down sulkily and wiped imaginary crumbs from the table. The ping of the microwave startled him. Lucy put the plate on the table and he stared at it for several moments.

'Aren't you going to eat it?'

'Yes, yes.' He picked up a fork and moved the food around as if looking for a rare insect specimen.

'What's wrong?'

Ian's head jerked up. 'Wrong?'

'With the food? You're gazing at it as if I'm trying to poison you.'

'No, it's – it's all right.'

'How do you know, you haven't tasted it?'

Ian quickly put a forkful of lasagne in his mouth and savoured it. 'It's lovely, Luce. You really are a good cook.'

The time between each mouthful became longer and longer.

'What was said that was so absorbing?' Ian frowned at Lucy. 'Your friend – what did he have to say?'

He pushed the plate away. 'I'm sorry, I can't eat this, I'm not hungry.'

'You didn't go to a pub, did you? You've been for a meal.'

'No Luce, honest.'

She knew he was lying. Lucy snatched his plate away and shot the food into the bin. 'I'm going to watch television,' she said.

'I'll get changed, shall I? Have a bath?'

'You do that.' She could hear the relief in his voice as she left him.

In the living room she stared unseeing at the TV as she had at her book. Added to the worry that Ian might have had an accident was a feeling of apprehension. Recently the clients he had to see after work seemed to have grown so numerous, Lucy wondered if he did anything during office hours.

Ian sidled into the room wearing his navy towelling bathrobe. He sat in the chair opposite Lucy and rubbed his damp hair, then sat fiddling with the towel. 'I was with Rebecca.'

'I guessed as much.'

Startled, he said, 'You did? How?'

'Because you would have told me straightaway. You're no good at lying. But you could have said, I wouldn't have minded. I know you have a lot in common with her.'

'I didn't know how to tell you – what to say.' Ian's eyes pleaded for her help.

In that one sentence Lucy saw it all. The late nights, sometimes just the next train, sometimes an hour, but not long enough to be discussing business with clients. Then there were the weekend sports conferences when he hadn't regaled her on his return, with how good or boring it had been. A sensation rose up Lucy's body like a fast incoming tide. It was the same sickening feeling she had when her mother was about to row with her. Lucy pushed her trembling hands into the pockets of her skirt, and with a calmness she did not feel, she said, 'Pretend you're telling me about a game you've just played.'

'Oh, Luce, I didn't mean this to happen.'

'That's a good cliché.'

'We just met – unexpectedly – in town one evening, and one thing led to another.'

'Cliché number two.'

Ian leapt up, his face flushed. 'You always think you're so superior – going to plays, reading boring books. Well, I play sport, that's nothing to be ashamed of. I don't beat up old ladies, take drugs or get drunk.'

'No, you don't do that,' she said, tears already brimming, 'but you don't mind having an affair behind my back.'

'I didn't want it to happen, really I didn't,' he repeated, sitting down again, 'but Rebecca and me – we get on so well. You're not interested in the same things.'

'You knew that before you asked me to move in with you.'

'I felt sorry for you.'

Lucy thought she couldn't be more hurt. The words cut into her. How right her mother had been all along. Nobody could love someone like her. Hadn't she been told enough times? She was just to be pitied. Poor, naïve Lucy to imagine someone might care. Tears fell and her throat hurt trying to hold them back. Lucy jumped from the chair.

'I'll just get a few things and fetch the rest some other time.'

'But you can't go now, it's late.'

'So?'

Ian followed her into the bedroom. 'But where will you go?'

'Dunno.'

'Stay here till the morning at least, Lucy. Please.'

'I can't – not now I know what you think of me.'

'I didn't mean what I said. We've had some good times, haven't we?' He put his hand on her shoulder but she shrugged it off.

'Why couldn't you have told me about Rebecca? Surely you owed me that much. We have been living together.'

'I didn't know how to without hurting you.'

'That was nice. What were you intending, that I kept house while you continued your – your fling?'

Lucy stretched for her case on top of the wardrobe. Ian got it down for her, cementing the inevitability of it all. She opened drawers and through her tears tried to think ahead. Underclothes, nightdress, clothes for work tomorrow. Ian watched as she went into the bathroom and filled her washing bag. He hovered like a naughty schoolboy waiting to be dismissed; but she was the one being dismissed.

'I wish you wouldn't go tonight.'

'I don't fancy sleeping on the settee.'

'But it's so late – there won't be any trains at this time of night.'

Lucy zipped the case and side-stepping Ian's outstretched hand, took it into the hall. 'I'll collect the rest of my things as soon as I know where I'll be. I'll keep my key for the time being if you don't mind, then I can get in when you're not here.'

*

'What's up, Princess?' He studied her face. 'You look awful. What's the matter? I was just going to bed.'

Lucy pushed past Ted and strode into the living room, tearing off her coat and throwing it at the armchair, where it slid to the floor. 'Ian's having an affair with that Rebecca woman, the one we met when we went on that ghastly skiing holiday.'

Ted fetched a chair and put it close to where Lucy had parked herself. He took her cold hands in his. 'Tell me about it, Princess.'

'He s-said, he f-felt s-sorry f-for me,' she gulped. 'I've l-left him.'

'Perhaps it's for the best in the long run, though you don't see it now.' He squeezed her hands.

'You never liked him, did you?'

'I didn't dislike him, I just thought he wasn't right for you.'

'Why didn't you say?' she cried.

'You'd made a big decision about leaving home, which you needed to make. It was right at the time and I wasn't to know it wouldn't work out. Anyway, would you have listened?'

'Why can't someone love me like you love my mother?'

'I love you, Lucy.'

'Like you love her.'

'Well, no, not quite the same.'

'Why can't you love me like that?' she demanded. Had she not been so upset, she would have laughed at the expression on Ted's face.

'Lucy! What are you saying?'

'You don't really care about me, do you? Nobody does.'

'Of course I do, you're very dear to me. But if it weren't for your mother's pigheadedness, Catherine would be living here in my house. Would you be saying these things if she were?'

Lucy thought she would. No one ever considered her feelings, so why should she care about anyone else? 'What do you see in her – she's horrible to you most of the time?'

'One of those inexplicable things,' Ted admitted. 'The chemistry's right, I suppose.'

'She doesn't love you,' Lucy said, wanting to hurt as she had been. 'She makes use of you. My mother never does anything unless she gets something out of it.'

'You're being silly now because things aren't going right for you,' Ted said as he stood up and replaced the chair against the wall.

'Aren't you going to offer me a drink?' she asked, sarcastically.

'I was almost thinking of asking you to leave.'

'I haven't anywhere to go.'

'Look, I know you're upset, but you'll soon get over it.'

'Oh, yes, and how do you know?'

'Why are you acting like this? It's not like you.'

'No. I'm the one that always gives in; the one who makes concessions; the one who says she's sorry when it isn't her fault.' Lucy picked up her coat from the floor and felt in the pocket for a handkerchief. 'Why did Ian have to deceive me like that? Why can't people tell me the truth? I'm even palmed off with vague stories about my father and what he was like – killed in a road accident, brown hair, blue eyes, blah, blah, blah.' Lucy glanced up and her eyes detected a strange guilty expression on Ted's face. Her eyes narrowed. 'You know something about him, don't you?'

'No, I don't,' he said, unconvincingly.

'You do, you do. I can tell.'

Over the years, as Lucy's questions about her unknown father had become more probing, so they were more cursorily dismissed. Once or twice she'd caught out her mother or grandmother with inconsistencies, but was too scared to challenge.

'She never mentions your father,' Ted said.

'But you know something, I can see it in your face.'

'I – I…'

'Tell me, tell me what you know.'

Helplessly Ted stared at her. 'It's for Catherine to tell you. I said I wouldn't.'

'So even you've been betraying me all these years. You know how much I've wanted to know about my father. How could you be such a hypocrite? How could you? You, of all people.' Lucy stuffed the handkerchief in her skirt and reached for her coat. 'I'm going,' she said.

'To your mother's?'

'That's the last place I'd go, I'd rather die.'

'But it's nearly one. You can stay here, if you like.'

'I don't want to see or speak to you again. I'll find a hotel or – or something.'

'At this time of night? Please don't go like this.'

How funny Ian and Ted wanted her to stay when they had just shattered all her dreams. 'I'll be all right, don't worry about me – not that you have.'

'That's not true. I've pleaded with Catherine to tell you more, but I'm in a difficult position.'

Lucy walked into the hall and opened the front door. 'I wouldn't like you to be in a difficult position.'

Ted said, 'Will you ring me? I want to know where you are. Please don't think unkindly of me.' The gate clanged. 'I care about you very much,' he called after her.

When she had left Ted punched out Catherine's number. 'Lucy's left Ian.'

'Lucy's what?' Catherine said, sleepily.

'Left Ian.'

'Couldn't you have told me that in the morning? Is she with you?'

'No, she wouldn't stay. There's something else. She knows you haven't been telling her the truth about her father.'

'What have you told her?' she snapped.

'I haven't told her anything, she's worked it out for herself. *"Oh what a tangled web we weave when first…"'*

'Don't give me all that literary guff.'

'I warned you this would happen eventually,' Ted said.

'If you haven't told her anything, what can she do?'

'I just wish you'd come clean.'

'Well, I don't want to, and that's the end of the matter.'

'Aren't you worried about her? It's the middle of the night, for heaven's sake.'

'She'll get in touch if she wants to – she's not a child.'

'You're an unfeeling cow,' Ted said, slamming down the phone.

*

Ted had first seen Lucy's mother at his evening class. He could hardly stop staring at her. Checking the entry forms he discovered

6

she was a Miss Catherine Daniels. He couldn't believe such a stunning looking woman was not married. His first efforts at asking her out were icily rejected. A lesser man would have been put off for good by her taciturn rebuffs, but he could not get her out of his mind, and pursued her with a determination that even surprised him. On the fourth time of asking, she agreed to have a drink when the class had finished. She was very cool, gave him no encouragement and after one drink, left him more unsettled than if she had not gone out with him at all. It was not until he saw her in a supermarket close to his home, that he found an excuse to try again.

'Miss Daniels, what a coincidence. Do you always shop here?'

Her eyes narrowed. 'You've not been following me, have you?'

'I live in Streatham, you don't.' Ted grinned. 'Are you sure you're not following me?'

A child came up and put a bag of sugar in the trolley. Timidly she asked, 'Can I get anything else, Mummy?'

'No,' she said sharply, and started to move away. 'Now you know.'

'Wait a minute.' Ted put a hand on her trolley. 'Now I know what?'

'That I have a child and I'm not married.'

'So?'

'I'm not free to go out for drinks or take hospitality I can't repay.'

'I'm not expecting to be repaid.'

'No?'

'Why are you so cynical?'

'Wouldn't you be, with a child to bring up and little money.'

'No, I don't think I would.' Ted smiled down at the little girl, her red hair caught back with an Alice band. Shyly she returned his smile.

'Look, we can't talk here,' he said as shoppers glared at them. 'Let's go up to Streatham Common. We can go in my car and then I'll take you back to Clapham. It is Clapham, isn't it? I remember from the register.'

Catherine was about to refuse when the child said wistfully, 'I've never been to Streatham Common.'

'There, that's settled,' Ted said quickly. 'I'll wait for you at the checkout.'

They walked from Leigham Court Road to the Rookery, the girl skipping ahead, then rushing back to exclaim over something that had caught her eye. At one point she put her tiny hand in Ted's, but took it away before he had time to grasp it.

Catherine told him that she was nearly eighteen when Lucy was born and that Lucy's father had been killed in a car accident before they could get married. After that she did not mention him again. It was not until they had been together for some months that Catherine let slip that he had not been killed.

'What does Lucy know?' he'd asked.

'What I first told you, that his name is Peter Evans and that he was killed in a car accident.'

'But doesn't she ask questions?'

'Constantly. I make up the answers.'

'What – everything?'

'Yes, everything – his name, where the accident took place, what he looked like.'

'But she must wonder,' he said, thinking about the shy little girl wanting to tie up the loose ends that made her what she was.

'Believe me she does. I tell her what I think she wants to know. So does my mother, not that she knows much.'

From that day Ted was never any the wiser, but his heart ached when he heard Lucy pleading to be told more about her father.

CHAPTER 2

Lucy had lain awake for what was left of the night, worrying over what it was Ted knew concerning her father. She'd always suspected something. Her grandmother was so cagey and Lucy could remember her whispering with her mother whenever she'd asked questions when she was little. Perhaps her father had been murdered and not killed. Or was he a murderer and in prison? Could her father still be alive? Tears squeezed from her eyes as she thought of the duplicity of the two people she held most dear. How could they all have been so cruel?

Lucy could hear the chink of crockery and soft voices coming from downstairs. There was a light tap on the door.

'Ah, you're awake.' Denise came over and sat down on the bed.

'I must get ready for work,' Lucy said, as she levered herself up and reached for her watch on the bedside table.

'You don't look fit enough. Let me ring and say you're not well.'

Lucy fell back on the pillow. 'I was exhausted last night, but I've hardly slept. Were your parents very angry about my turning up like that?'

'No, of course not. Mum could see you were upset.'

'I'm sorry to…' Lucy burst into tears and grabbed the edge of the sheet to push into her eyes.

Denise put an arm round her. 'Look, I'll take the day off, I've time owing to me, then you can tell me all about it.'

Lucy protested. 'No, you mustn't do that.'

'Have you had a row with Ian?'

'He's carrying on with that woman he once knew, you know Rebecca, the one we met in France.'

'Did he tell you that?'

'It all came out in the end, but he was too much of a coward to tell me.' Lucy's lips trembled. 'And he said he'd only asked me to move in with him 'cause he felt sorry for me. Wasn't I the stupid one to think that anyone would want to love me just 'cause I'm me?'

'Of course someone will love you one day, Lucy.'

'But that's not all. I went to Ted's house before I came here and I said something about my father and there was this look on his face. I can't explain it, but I could tell he was hiding something. When I challenged him, he said – he said he'd promised my mother he wouldn't say anything. What d'you think Ted knows? Do you think my father could still be alive?' Lucy wiped her residue tears on the sheet.

Denise gave her a hug. 'I'm as shocked as you are about whatever it is they're not telling you. I haven't known you all these years without realising how much not having a father has meant to you. What are you going to do now?'

'Go to Nana's. I didn't go last night because it was so late, but I want to get to the bottom of this.'

'Are you sure…'

'What d'you mean, am I sure? Don't you want me to find out about him either?'

'Calm down, I was going to say are you sure you don't want me to take the day off?'

'I'm sorry, I'm a bit stressed out.'

'That's the understatement of the year.'

Lucy sat up. 'I will take the day off.' Her eyes searched around for her handbag and Denise handed it to her. She reached in and handed her a card.

'Ring my office and ask for Mr Constant. He'll probably sound grumpy but don't take any notice. Make it convincing and let me know what you say, so we get our stories straight – just like they all did. And if Ted rings, you know nothing.'

*

Ted's seventh years had been a model class. They were keen and asked intelligent questions about the book they were reading, but today their liveliness irritated him and instead of taking advantage, he had been unintentionally impatient. It was little better with the next class, so by the end of the day he didn't feel anything like coaching Lorraine and John.

Ted had hardly slept thinking about Lucy, and before he left for school he rang Catherine's mother who told him she'd not seen her. Surely Lucy hadn't wandered the streets all night? He wanted to start searching for her – but where?

Ted returned to his classroom where he found Lorraine waiting for him.

'John coming?'

'He said he was last time I saw him. He don't seem very interested, does he, Sir?'

'So I've noticed.'

The cleaner called from the corridor. 'Shall I shut your door? I'll be using the polisher soon and it makes a racket.'

'No, leave it open.'

'Please yourself,' the cleaner muttered, 'but it'll be noisy.'

John came into the room, shirt half out, tie crooked, swinging his bag which banged into a desk.

'Must you do that? Get a chair and sit down.'

Ted sat behind his own desk and reached for a book on the shelf beside him.

'Is that essay ready? You were going to give it to me yesterday. I could have marked it last night and gone through it now.'

John handed him two sheets of crumpled paper, which Ted scanned.

'There are barely four sides here. That all you could manage?'

John tipped back his chair. 'Yes, Sir.'

'Sit up. Look, there's no point in my wasting time giving you extra lessons if you're not going to put some effort into it.'

'I didn't want to stay at school anyway, it was my Dad's idea.'

'I gathered that at the Parents' Meeting, and I did try to put your point of view.'

'But you told them I could pass with a bit of extra work, so me old man got all keen again.'

'I did say that, and you can, but I'm doing the extra work and you're hardly doing anything.'

'Can't you talk to him again. Tell him I'm hopeless.'

'You're not hopeless, but I will talk to your Group Tutor. What about the other subjects you're taking?'

'I'm re-taking a couple of GCSEs and 'A' level sociology.'

'He ain't much good at that either,' Lorraine volunteered.

John glared at her. 'What's it got to do with you, mind your own business.'

'I'm sorry, John, but while you're in school, I expect you to work. Lorraine doesn't find it easy, but she is trying. Can't the two of you work together sometimes?'

11

Lorraine's smug smile instantly turned to one of derision. 'I don't want to work with him.'

Ted opened his mouth to tell her she should do as she was told, but muttered instead, *'With native humour tem'pring virtuous rage.'''*

'What's that, Sir?' Lorraine asked.

'Just a quotation.' Ted put a hand to his thumping head and closed his eyes. 'Right,' he opened his book. 'Let's get going before the cleaner flies in on her broomstick.'

*

'Hello, Lucy love,' her grandmother said as she let her in. 'Ted rang 'bout you. He was worried. What you been doing? Shouldn't you be at work?'

'I've taken the day off, Nana. I want to talk to you.'

'What's the matter?' She peered at her granddaughter. 'You don't look very well. Come into the kitchen and I'll put the kettle on.'

'I want to know about my father.'

'Oh dear, Ted said you'd guessed something when he rang. But what about your mother? She'll be …'

'What about my mother! I want to know the truth once and for all.'

'It wasn't my idea,' her grandmother said, looking uncomfortable, 'I would have told you everything – well as much as I knew.' Lucy's voice broke as she said, bitterly, 'But you all did as you were told.'

Mrs Daniels put her arm round her. 'I – I don't know what to say dear.'

'You can start with the true story.'

'As I said, I don't know much.'

'Everything, Nana, everything you know I want to hear.'

'Your mother used to like dancing,' her grandmother began, staring at Lucy as if seeing her for the first time. 'She would go anywhere that was holding one. Sometimes she would go with friends or the current boyfriend – she had plenty of those. At one of these dances she met a fellow.'

'And that was my father?'

'Your Grandpa and I assumed so; we never met him.'

Lucy raised her eyebrows. 'But – but you used to tell me what he looked like and – and everything.'

'I couldn't bear not to answer your questions, so I used to ask your mother about his appearance and tell you as if I knew.'

Lucy closed her eyes, crushed by these disclosures.

'Are you sure you're not ill, dear?'

'I haven't had much sleep – go on.'

'She never brought this chap home, you see, but I knew about him; knew Catherine was keen. They'd go dancing, uptown in the West End. Your Grandpa kept asking her to bring him home. He didn't like her being so thick with someone we hadn't met. And she was only just seventeen.'

'So you say you never saw my father?'

'No, never.'

'How old was he?'

'I've no idea. I always took him to be around your Mum's age early twenties maybe.'

Mrs Daniels carefully placed their cups and saucers on the table, before saying, 'One evening your mother came home very tearful.'

'Tearful!' Lucy exclaimed. The sight of her mother in tears was hard to picture.

'She'd been behaving strangely for some time, but your mother was always an awkward child, so we hadn't taken too much notice. On this particular evening she told me she was expecting a baby and that this Peter Evans was the father. Your grandfather was very angry and wanted to go and sort him out, but your mother said she wasn't going to see him any more and didn't even know his address. Your grandfather didn't believe her, but I think she may have been telling the truth – about not knowing his address, I mean.'

'Was he already married do you think?'

'I don't know that either. Not very likely if he was still in his teens or early twenties. The affair, if that's what you'd call it, hadn't lasted long. Your mother said your father would send money to support you – and he did for a while.'

'So, he wasn't killed in an accident?' Lucy's whole body shook as she thought of the lies she had been told. She had a right to know, didn't they realise that?

'He stopped sending money, didn't he, about the time I went to school?'

Mystified, her grandmother said, 'How did you know that if you thought he was dead?'

'Something I've dredged from my kiddy mind. Do you have any idea where he lived?'

'Catherine once let slip that his family lived in South London, I think Crystal Palace way, but don't ask me how I know that. I'm pretty sure she never met his parents. She only met this chap in town as far as we could gather.'

'If he lived so close to us, wouldn't she have come across him?'

Her grandmother shook her head. 'I'm certain she never did.'

'And the money?'

'It was paid into an account. When the money stopped, your mother wrote to the bank but they wouldn't give her any information. And that's all I know – honestly.'

Lucy put her hand to her forehead, turning these new facts over in her mind and trying to sort out her feelings. Her father was alive, or maybe dead if the money stopped. Perhaps the money ceased because he was ill, or had no job. More likely, he no longer cared about the daughter he'd never seen because, as her mother said, nobody could love her.

'Why on earth couldn't my mother tell me all this? What was the point of letting me think he'd died in an accident?'

'I've no idea. Your mother is a law unto herself - always has been. I've asked her, but she'd never give a reason.' Her grandmother looked worried. 'I'll never hear the end of this when she finds out what I've told you.'

It didn't take much imagination on Lucy's part to know how she felt. 'I no longer care what she thinks. Is there anything else you know?'

'Nothing, love, really. I used to beg her to tell you, but she insisted we all stick to her story.'

A desperate tiredness overcame her. 'Nana, can I stay here for a few days?'

'Of course, darling, for as long as you like.'

'Do you mind if I go and lie down now? I can't keep my eyes open any longer.'

Lucy picked up her small case and handbag. 'If Ted rings again, tell him you haven't seen me. The same goes for Mum, not that she's likely to be bothered.'

*

Lucy woke suddenly, knowing there was something wrong, but couldn't immediately remember what. A feeling of utter desolation overcame her as if there were no one else in the world. Then the events of the last twenty-four hours permeated her consciousness –

Ian, Ted and her grandmother's revelations. Her whole body felt empty – drained of blood. Lifeless.

Lucy put on the bedside light, illuminating the familiar room. This had been her home for the first two years of her life, but Nana had looked after her when she and her mother had moved to their own place. She slowly gazed round the room catching sight of her hatpin collection. Nana had found three pretty hatpins that had belonged to her grandmother and had bought Lucy three more and a holder for them. Lucy had forgotten all about them as she rarely came into this bedroom.

A photo on a chest of drawers was of her grandparents. Her grandfather was a vague figure, large to her child eyes with ginger hair that she and her mother had inherited. Perhaps her father had red hair, too. Brown and curly was what she'd been told, but then her mother was probably lying. She would lie about anything if she thought it would make Lucy miserable.

'Nana,' she said, as she went into the kitchen. 'I'm going to look for my father.'

CHAPTER 3

Ted went straight to the phone when he reached home. While it rang he shook his arm out of his coat, changed hands and let the coat drop to the floor.

'Hello, Mrs Daniels, it's Ted again. Has Lucy turned up?'

'No.' There was a slight pause. 'No, she hasn't turned up here. I wonder where she could've got to?'

'I'm worried about her. She was very upset last night.'

'Well, I haven't seen her. If I do I'll tell you.'

Ted slumped into an armchair wondering what to do next. He sat forward suddenly. Denise, of course. He fell back unable to remember her surname? His anxiety overcame his reluctance to ring Catherine. He picked up the phone then slammed that down, remembering she wouldn't be home from work yet.

He was sick with apprehension and wished he'd told Lucy what he knew about her father – not that there was much to tell. He also wished he hadn't let her drift off into the night. He wished … he wished ….

*

Ted watched enviously as members of staff left for home, even though he knew they probably carried several hours of work in their cases. He still had no news of Lucy and a week had gone by.

Lorraine bounced into the room announcing gaily. 'John's not coming.'

'Oh, what's his excuse this time?'

'He finally got his father to let him leave at Easter, so he said there weren't much point.'

'I suppose it would've been too much to come and tell me himself,' Ted said, feeling he had to vent his annoyance on someone.

Lorraine shrugged. 'But we'll be able to get on much better with him not 'ere, won't we, Sir?' She fetched a chair and put it beside his. 'Just the two of us.'

'I think you'd be better sitting where you usually do.'

'Oh, Sir, I sat beside you once when you were explaining something.'

'I prefer you to sit there.' Ted pointed to the other side of his desk and with a clatter she moved the chair and sat petulantly.

'I want to go over the poem I read at the end of the lesson on Wednesday.'

'To tell you the truth, I thought it a load of rubbish. All about fleas.' She pulled a face.

'Sitting looking at me won't help.' Ted gave her what he thought was a smile of encouragement. 'Get your book out.'

'I like looking at you, Mr Lassiter.' Lorraine smiled dreamily.

This is all he needed – a girl with a crush on him.

Mrs Daniels saying that she'd not seen Lucy sounded too unconcerned. Catherine hadn't been in touch and he was damned if he was going to ring her again. Eventually he remembered Denise's name and phoned, but she said Lucy wasn't staying there and didn't know where she was. He couldn't be sure she was telling the truth either, but she did suggest he rang Lucy's office and gave him the number. They only confirmed that she was at work and personal calls were not allowed. It was some relief to know she hadn't been mugged and wasn't lying in hospital. The end of term fatigue, the lack of response from Catherine, his concern for Lucy and now this lovesick teenager were making life intolerable.

'Lorraine,' Ted admonished, 'you're in school to learn, not moon over someone old enough to be your grandfather.'

She laughed. 'You're not old enough to be me grandfather, you're about the same age as me Dad.'

'I read this poem last lesson,' Ted went on, ignoring her remark, 'because I wanted the class to think about it before I covered it in detail next time. This is a love poem...' he began.

'A love poem!' she exclaimed, laughing, 'about fleas. You're 'aving me on.'

'John Donne uses comparisons, called conceits, to show the likeness of two things that don't seem to be alike.' Lorraine looked unconvinced. 'What he says is that he and his beloved have been bitten by a flea so their blood is mingled together inside it.

> *"This flea is you and I, and this*
> *Our marriage bed, and marriage temple is."*

Now, read it through to yourself and tell me what you think he's saying.'

Ted followed her eyes as they flitted from side to side. 'Well?'

he queried when she'd finished.

'Is he trying to seduce her by telling her that the mingling of blood means they're as good as married?'

'Now has that made it seem less like rubbish?'

'The dirty devil. Fancy writing about something like that.' Lorraine gave him a saucy grin. 'I didn't understand it at all in class but now you've explained it to me, it's ever so much clearer.'

'Good, you've done well. Now you've got the gist of it we'll go through it once more, then I'll look at your Shakespeare essay.'

Twenty minutes later, Ted closed his book. 'Right, this is our last lesson before we break up for Easter. Next term I think you can go it alone.'

Lorraine shot out of her chair. 'You can't give up on me now,' she cried, aghast. 'I'm doing so well – you just said. You told John I was trying hard and I am.'

'I'm not giving up on you Lorraine, but you've a better understanding of what's expected at this level, and if you go on working as hard as you have been, then you'll pass.'

She started to cry. 'I thought you cared about me.'

Ted had a feeling of déjà vu. 'Come on, time you went home.'

He replaced the anthology in the bookcase and picked up his jacket from the back of the chair.

'So that's what I get for all the hard work I've put in.'

'What you get for the hard work you do is a pass at 'A' level and, I hope, a greater love of literature.'

The cleaner came into the room from the corridor where she had been clattering for the last five minutes. He smiled at her and said, 'We're just off out of your way.'

*

Lucy climbed the carpet-worn stairs. Tomorrow was Good Friday and she was anticipating a few days' peace so she could gather her thoughts and set about finding her father. Mr Constant, a hard taskmaster at the best of times, had been particularly cantankerous and found pernickety fault with everything she did. Lucy thought it wouldn't be worth studying to be a legal executive if this was going to be her life till he retired.

The shabby bedsit, the best she had found for the money she could afford, was on the top floor of a turn of the century house in Lewisham. Cheap, but relatively new, brown cord carpet covered the floor of her room. There was a sink and draining board in one corner and beside it a tabletop electric cooker. Over this were two kitchen cupboards. By the window, set into the sloping wall, was a table, once well polished, but now covered in interlocking rings, which reminded Lucy of the Olympic flag. Three chairs were tucked tidily underneath. Two small fireside chairs with greasy arms were placed either side of an electric fire. Against another wall were a put-u-up and a side table with a portable television set on it. The fourth wall had a wardrobe where Lucy now hung her coat.

She removed the pot plant from the centre of the table and spread out the evening papers she had bought on the way home, and searched through the personal columns. There was nothing there to help with the wording of her advert. She grabbed paper and pencil and wrote –

Does anyone know the whereabouts of
a Peter Evans, aged

Lucy put the end of her pencil in her mouth and tapped her teeth. What age? Same as her mother? Could hardly have been younger if he had a job and money to send for her upkeep. Her grandmother thought he was in his twenties at that time. She crossed out aged and put –

last heard of in South London possibly
the Crystal Palace area, 1976/77

She shook her head and started again.

I am trying to trace a Peter Evans: family
last heard of in South London possibly in
the Crystal Palace area mid seventies.
PO Box

That sounded better. Lucy wrote it out three times, and put each one in an envelope addressed to three newspaper offices. She propped them against the pot plant on the table and stared at them. Perhaps she would go to the post now instead of in the morning. The sooner she could trace her father, the better.

For the next fortnight Lucy anxiously awaited replies. She had all but given up when a large envelope awaited her when she came home from work. With fingers that would hardly obey her, she ran her thumb along the envelope and tipped out the contents. Inside were two letters, one from a man in his eighties giving his life history from the day he was born. Disappointed, Lucy dropped it on the table and snatched the other one. She tore at the cheap manila envelope and pulled out a sheet that had been torn from an exercise book. She only read two lines. It was so disgusting, she screwed it up and chucked it in the bin.

Lucy sat on her bed twirling her bracelet. Was this all her life would be, living in this one room? Denise had her Tony, Ted had Catherine but there was no one who cared what happened to her. Even the thought of the exams she was working towards seemed far away and pointless. Tears trickled down her face.

Another week went by with no replies and dispirited, Lucy wondered what she could do next. But one evening a letter from another of the newspapers was waiting in the hall. Lucy read the letter, excitement mounting, as she climbed to her room. This is it, she told herself. Answering straightaway, she took it up to the newspaper office by hand. When she received a letter in reply, she rushed round to Denise.

'I wrote immediately to the address he gave, but I didn't say why I wanted to know about him,' she explained to Denise, her face flushed. 'I asked if I could meet him at his house and he wrote back suggesting next Saturday. Isn't it exciting?'

'I don't know about exciting. Don't you think you're being a bit reckless? You weren't intending to go alone, were you?'

Lucy's face fell. 'I hadn't thought. I suppose it would be silly.'

'You might be intelligent, Lucy, but you do do some daft things at times. I'll come with you, if you like.'

'Would you? That'll be great.'

'What did he say in his letter?'

'His name is Peter Evans, and his home has been in the Crystal Palace area since he was born.'

'Did he say how old he was?'

'No, but he sounds the right sort of age.'

Denise laughed. 'How can you tell that from a letter?'

'Oh, it must be right, it must be.'

*

It was a grey, dismal day. Litter blew about in the wind, but Lucy didn't notice. They walked past the buses lined up on either side of the Parade, idling engines belching out fumes. The television transmitter towered over them as they walked briskly along the wide road. Lucy studied the rough plan the man had drawn for her.

'We turn left down there by the lights.' She pointed ahead. 'That should be College Road.' She consulted the paper again. 'Then we go up one of the turnings called Hilton Road.'

When they reached the house they both stood outside open-mouthed. It was detached, double-fronted, with a bay window downstairs on one side. The upstairs windows had mock shutters and there were two garages on the left, and a small front garden.

'This looks a bit posh,' Denise said.

'There's nothing that says my father couldn't have been a wealthy man,' Lucy said, haughtily.

'I didn't mean that. I just meant this isn't what I call Crystal Palace. It's more like Dulwich.'

As Denise rang the bell, Lucy's eyes were fixed on the door. She straightened her skirt and patted her hair, which she'd put up to make herself look more like her mother. The door was opened and a tall man stood there, his blue eyes looking quizzically at them. He wore an open-necked, navy check shirt, jeans and trainers.

'Miss Daniels?' He looked from one to the other.

'I – I'm Lucy Daniels.' She stared at him, wide-eyed with anticipation, waiting for him to say some magic words like *"you must be Catherine's daughter"*.

'And this is?' he turned to Denise.

'I'm Lucy's friend, Denise Gannon.' She held out her hand.

Peter Evans shook it and moved his hand towards Lucy, but let it drop as she continued staring at his face.

'Come in,' he said, leading them through to a comfortable, but conservatively furnished drawing room to the left of the hall. He motioned the girls to a settee. When they were seated, he said, 'I was intrigued by the advertisement.' A quirky smile played round his lips as he surveyed the pair. 'I wasn't going to reply, but curiosity got the better of me. So – what can I do for you?'

Lucy burst out, 'I think you may be my father.'

*

'Whatever possessed you to say that?' Denise rounded on Lucy when they had departed from Peter Evans' house. 'Couldn't you see he was much too young to be your father. I was so embarrassed.'

Mortified, and close to tears, Lucy said, 'I'd so made up my mind it would be him.'

They retraced their steps and waited for their bus.

'Look, I haven't said this before, but the chances of finding your father are pretty remote. Knowing your mother, she probably lied about where his family lived. Your grandmother, you said, wasn't sure herself. He could be anywhere in the country – even abroad.' Denise weighed her words and gently, she said, 'If the money stopped suddenly, it could be because your father had died.

'I know, I have tried to be realistic, but I still want to know about him, even if he is dead.'

'But you have so little to go on, and it's a long time ago now. Are you sure your grandmother has told you everything? If your mother always made things up, your father's name is not likely to be Evans, or Peter come to that. What about asking your mother again?'

'I wouldn't ask and she wouldn't tell me anyway.' Lucy knew her mother would delight in knowing she was searching for her father and would enjoy giving her nothing but misinformation.

'Then I think you ought to face facts and give up. Concentrate on getting the qualifications you're working towards, then you'll be earning decent money and can move out of that awful place. You'll meet a nice young man who'll sweep you off your feet and you'll live happily ever after.'

Their bus drew up and they climbed on to the 137 and went upstairs. Lucy walked to the front seat and sat down, saying, 'And there'll be lots of little Lucys who won't need to look for their father.'

'Quite right,' her friend replied, giving Lucy a pat.

'If you think that's best.'

'I do, I really do.' Lucy went to speak. 'No buts, think positive, as they say.'

'Ungrammatically,' Lucy added laughing.

*

Lucy turned to the portable television that was placed, for want of a socket in a better position, on the bedside table. She switched on. It flickered and rolled and eventually a highly-coloured, wavering picture of a tennis court and luridly dressed spectators arranged itself on the screen. She tried all the stations till she was back with the tennis.

What a mess her life was. It must be her fault. If she hadn't gone on and on about her father, no one would have had to deceive her. She wished Denise could have stayed with her this afternoon; she wanted to stop thinking about how lonely and unhappy she was – to stop thinking altogether, if that were possible.

'Fifteen-forty,' declared the umpire, his chair swaying ominously. Perhaps he'll fall out, she thought.

Ian and Rebecca would be playing this afternoon. She pictured them now, Ian running round the court his racquet an extension of his arm, eyes alert, muscles taut with exertion –

Rebecca the other end, tall and willowy, hair flying in the breeze, hardly breaking into a sweat. They would rush to the net and he would kiss her like he used to kiss Lucy, and they would walk arm in arm to the clubhouse, discussing every point. Lucy would have said "well played" and he would have explained every point.

'Deuce,' the swaying umpire said, and the crowd clapped rapturously. Tears rolled down her cheeks, which she made no move to wipe away. The bell above her door buzzed, startling her. Wrong flat yet again. Annoyed she trudged down the stairs ready to give the caller a lesson in reading nameplates.

'Mr Evans! What on earth are you doing here?'

He was dressed more formally than earlier that morning – cream shirt, fawn trousers, brown shoes. He carried a leather jacket over his shoulder, a finger through the loop.

'Peter please – or would you rather call me Father.'

Lucy's face was hot and she knew she had blushed and he would see what an incredibly stupid woman she was. 'My – I mean I'm – my behaviour was quite appalling. I'm so sorry to have embarrassed you like that.'

Peter stood waiting. 'May I come in?' he said, at last. He gave a smile that lifted the corners of his mouth.

Lucy wondered what Denise would say. No, she really must stand by her own decisions. She had already met him after all. 'It's not much of a place,' she said, apologetically, as she led him through the cluttered hall and up the three flights of stairs.

Peter glanced at the television. 'Do you like tennis?'

'Not much.'

'Why have you got it on then?'

'Dunno, just something to look at.'

'You've been crying?' Lucy put her hand to her cheek about to protest. 'There's nothing wrong with crying if you're upset. Was it because I wasn't who you thought I was?'

'Partly.'

'Do you want to talk about it?'

'I wouldn't want to bore you,' Lucy said, as Peter took the chair opposite hers. 'Why are you here? Did we leave something?'

'I felt sorry for you,' he said.

'Ah, yes. Everyone feels sorry for me. That's about all they do.'

'Could we turn that thing off? I don't know how you can look at such a dreadful picture.' Without waiting for an answer, he went over to the TV.

'The set was here when I came,' Lucy said. 'I've thought about getting another, but I don't watch much television.'

'How long have you lived here?'

Lucy saw him gazing about the room no doubt thinking how disgusting it was. What would he think about her living in such squalor?

'Three weeks.'

'Where were you before that?'

This man is very inquisitive, Lucy thought, as she studied him more closely. He really did resemble the description her mother had made up – blue eyes, wavy brown hair. Pity that's where it ended.

'How old are you?' Lucy asked.

'I'm thirty-two.'

'That is too young to be my father. I'm twenty-one.'

'Why were you crying?'

Lucy sighed. 'The tennis reminded me of my ex-boyfriend. He was keen on tennis and rugby and football and anything else that involved flinging himself about wildly.'

'And you weren't?'

'No, but I was quite happy to go and watch him.'

'Is that why you split up?'

'He found someone else.'

'And she played sport?'

'And was tall, slim and beautiful. What more could he want?'

'You're beautiful.'

'Oh yes? Is that your usual chat-up line?' Lucy gave him a wry smile. This man would need watching.

Peter Evans looked miffed. 'I mean it, and when I said I felt sorry for you, I meant I was upset to see you so unhappy.'

'You haven't told me why you're here?'

'I thought I might be able to help you.'

'Help me do what?'

'Search for your father. It's obviously important to you.'

Lucy's heart leapt, then she thought of Denise's comments.

'My friend thinks it's a wild goose chase and I should give up the idea.'

'And what do you think?'

For the first time Lucy had a sympathetic ear - someone who knew nothing about her and who would judge her as she was now - not as an intelligent schoolgirl as Ted did, nor an unlovable nuisance like her mother did, nor a pathetic dipstick like everyone else.

'Have you a couple of days to spare?'

When she had finished her tale, Lucy said, 'So you see, that's why I want to find out about my father, even if he is dead?'

Peter moved to sit at the table by the window and gazed out for so long she thought he'd fallen asleep.

'Peter?'

'Did you love this Ian?'

It was Lucy's turn to contemplate the rooftops as she moved to sit opposite and rested her elbows on the table. 'No, not really. I thought I did, but I think it was gratitude I felt. He was a means of escape from my mother and he gave me the attention I craved which I thought was love. I was fond of him.' She shrugged. 'It wasn't any wonder he found someone else, was it?'

Peter jumped up nearly tipping the chair. 'I'm starving. Let me take you out to dinner.'

They went to a restaurant in Bromley. Lucy was childishly thrilled. She had never been anywhere quite as smart as this.

'I work in a solicitor's office. I'm studying to be a legal executive.' she told him over the soup, hoping to impress. 'But the man they've put me with is hard to please.'

'I bet you cope with him, you seem so calm.'

Lucy was about to deny this but decided she was no longer going to put herself down. If he thought she was calm, she was calm, and if he thought she was beautiful, she was beautiful, even though she knew she wasn't.

'Now you can tell me your life history,' Lucy said.

'Boring, boring.'

Lucy thought Peter's life far from boring. His father had owned an electrical business, which he and his partner had built up from scratch. Peter's parents wanted him to go to university and then join the company but, to their disgust, he left midway through his 'A' level and went to sea. Then he got a job on the oilrigs, but when his father died his mother begged him to come home for good and take over.

'Did you want to?' Lucy asked.

'Yes and no. I liked the independence of the rigs and the money was good, but I didn't want to see the business my father had started fold up, or be taken over – so duty called.'

'No girlfriends?' She might as well know now if there were

any Rebeccas lurking in the background.

'Plenty, but nothing lasting. I was away for months on end and they didn't want to hang around.'

'And since you've been home?'

'Too busy, it takes a long time to pick up the reins of a business you know nothing about. I was lucky that it was well run because my father had a partner who had known me since I was born. My way was smooth to a certain extent. But I still had to learn.'

Lucy surreptitiously glanced round the restaurant. A family of four, smartly dressed, was at the next table and on their other side a couple sitting side by side touching each other at every opportunity. They looked very much in love.

'You look just as nice as anyone else here, you know.'

'You knew what I was thinking.'

'You're a bit transparent.'

Lucy's face fell. Now he would know how unsophisticated she was. Transparent? Was that another flaw to add to her other imperfections?

'I expect you're used to this type of restaurant. I've never eaten anywhere as nice as this. Ian and I used to go to an Italian in Soho sometimes and we went to the local café where we lived, but Ian was always training or playing, so we didn't eat out much.'

'He sounds like a right pain in the nether regions.'

Lucy laughed. 'He was a bit.' She felt relieved she could say this and have an understanding confidante.

'I think you had a narrow escape and he did you a favour.'

'I'm beginning to think the same.'

CHAPTER 4

Kate Doggett pushed open the swing door of the staff room. It was the first day of term, one of the few times so many teachers assembled in one room. Some stood sorting through their papers, or scanning the notice board for anything pristine that had not been left curling and dusty from the previous term. Others gathered in small knots comparing the merits of Corfu with those of Cefalonia. The level of noise was such that would not have been tolerated in their classrooms.

'Who d'you want?' Kate was asked, as she searched the faces.

'Ted Lassiter.'

'Over there, talking to Richard.'

Kate elbowed her way through, and tapped Ted on the shoulder. 'The Head wants to see you straightaway.'

'OK.' He turned to his friend. 'Catch you later. Glad you and Sheila had a good time.'

'You come as well,' she said to Richard.

Puzzled, they followed the secretary out of the staff room and made their way along the corridor thronged with jostling children doing much the same as their elders, only several decibels higher.

'Ted, Richard, sit down.' Stephen Holloway indicated the chairs in front of his desk. 'This is Gerald Manser, the Area Personnel Manager from the LEA.'

They shook hands. Ted had never met the man before though he knew of his existence. What could he want with them?

'I've, er – I've had a complaint – from Mr and Mrs Cromer.'

'What have I done? Given Lorraine too much work, or not enough?' Ted laughed. 'They're the usual complaints. Richard in the same boat?'

'It's a bit more serious than that I'm afraid.'

Ted searched his mind for what could be as serious as the Head appeared. Stephen's face was strained and not like that of a man just returning from a two-week break.

'Is it because I said I wasn't going to give her any more help after school? I knew she was annoyed.'

'She told her parents you had been molesting her.'

Ted's mouth dropped open and for a few seconds he felt he was watching a play and that this could not be happening to him.

'Molesting her! What does she mean by that?'

'That's what we have to find out. Meantime, I'll have to suspend you because of the seriousness of the allegation.'

Ted stared at the Head with incredulity. Glancing at Richard, Ted saw that his friend was looking like he felt. 'And what's Richard got to do with it? Has he also been accused?'

'No, it's part of the procedure. It's usual to have a colleague present. You can, of course, contact your Union representative.'

'But what about my classes. My GCSE class has exams soon, and my 'A' level one.'

'That's the least of your worries at the moment. I'll have to inform the Governors and there'll be an enquiry. But I have to ask you – are there any grounds for this complaint?'

'No there bloody well isn't! I knew the girl had a crush on me, but I ignored her – like I always do.'

'Were you ever alone with her?'

'Not by design. I had John Denny as well, but once he didn't turn up and he didn't bother to come at the end of last term because he was leaving.'

'Yes, I see.' The Head, clearly uncomfortable, moved papers around his desk.

'I've been teaching a long time, Stephen. I wouldn't let myself be in a compromising situation, you know that.'

'I don't doubt you, but these things have to take their course.'

'When was I supposed to have done – whatever she says I've done?'

'They didn't say. I only received their letter yesterday. They're coming in this afternoon.'

'What do I do now?' Ted asked, wanting desperately to get to his class.

'Collect what you want and go home. Stay there till I get in touch.'

'But my classes! I can't desert them now.'

'I'll get Michael to re-arrange them and we'll have to get in a supply teacher.'

'But...'

'Ted, go home. If you've done nothing wrong, it'll soon be

sorted out.'

'What d'you mean if,' he said angrily. 'You know it's all lies. I'd never, ever do anything like that.'

'I understand how you feel, but I've got to follow the rules.'

'Rules,' Ted spat out, 'And meanwhile my pupils are suffering at the most important time in their school careers, just because some love-sick teenager wants to stir up trouble.'

The Head stood up. 'I don't doubt you and I'm as sorry about this as you are. I'll ring you later when I've seen the Cromers and you've had time to – to – and I'll tell you the course we must take. Meanwhile, I'll confirm this meeting in writing.'

They rose from their chairs and Ted could see the sympathy in Stephen's eyes, but his stance implied he wished Ted were elsewhere – and the quicker the better.

The journey home seemed interminable, though in reality it took him half the time it did in the rush hour. He went over in his mind all that he had said to the girl. The only physical contact was when she had put her hand on his, and that had been weeks ago. Damn the girl. Damn all women, he said to himself as he banged the garage door shut.

Ted fetched a bottle of whisky from the sideboard where it had lain untouched since Christmas. He put it on the coffee table and went to the dining room where he retrieved the cigarettes that Catherine had hidden.

'Hasn't worked, darling,' he muttered as he went back into the living room. Carefully he measured out a whisky, studied it, and added the same again and settled into his chair.

Ted thought he ought to open his eyes, but he couldn't be bothered. If that noise were a burglar, he would have to burgle. He heard the front door shut and Catherine burst into the room.

'What on earth have you been doing?' she exclaimed, surveying the mess around him.

With eyes still closed Ted reached down beside the chair and felt the air till his fingers found the empty bottle. He grasped it by the neck and waved it in the air like a trophy. A few drops splashed on to his face. Catherine frowned at the stubs in the ashtray and the long finger of ash of a burned down cigarette.

'How long have you been home?' she demanded.

'Hou-ers and hou-ers and hou-ers.'

'You're drunk.'

'Well desused - desdussed - seduced.' He giggled.

Catherine took off her coat and tossed it in the chair. She picked up the bottle and glass in one hand and the ashtray in the other and, holding them at arms' length, took them into the kitchen.

'Had anything to eat?' she called.

She returned to find Ted asleep. She grabbed his shoulders and his head wobbled like a rag doll as she shook him.

'Wha's up?' he mumbled, peering at her through slitted eyes. 'Oh, ishu, another bloody woman to make my life a misery.'

Catherine wrinkled her nose. 'You stink. Go up and shower.' She tried unsuccessfully to pull him out of the chair.

'I suppose you haven't eaten for hours and hours either?'

'Nope.' He fell back.

Five minutes later she was holding his head while he drank from a mug of strong coffee.

'Right, now let's get you upstairs.' Catherine hauled him out of the armchair and he stood swaying like a sapling in the breeze. She put his arm round her neck and struggled with him up the stairs. Propping him against the bathroom wall, she fumbled with his tie.

'I don't know what you've been doing?' she said, as she fought with the tight knot, 'but I don't suppose I'll get any sense out of you till you've sobered up. There.' She threw the tie on the bathroom floor and unbuttoned his shirt.

'You could get into trouble for thish, you know. You're molesting me. Really, really molesting me.' Ted shook his head from side to side like an elephant. 'You're inviding my pravicy.'

'Shut up and get the rest of your clothes off.'

'Are you coming in with me?'

'No I'm not.'

'Shame.' He swung his leg over the bath unable to work out why he was kneeling instead of sitting. While still puzzling Catherine, shower in hand, turned the tap on full blast, and swished it up and down his crouching form. Ted let out a yell of anguish as the icy deluge splashed over him. He cowered low and covered his head with his hands as if this would offer protection. 'Stop, Catherine, stop.' His agonised cry rose. 'I'll do whatever you say. You're killing me.'

She turned off the tap. 'You're such a baby. Here.' She threw a bathrobe from the back of the door. 'I'm going to get something to eat. By that time, perhaps you'll be in a fit state to tell me what's been going on.'

*

Ted's head thumped like a ship's engine as he picked at the scrambled egg put in front of him.

'Eat it,' Catherine ordered.

'I can't, I'll be sick.'

'No you won't, you'll feel better when you've got something inside you to mop up the alcohol.'

'My God, Catherine, no wonder Lucy left home, you're even worse than I thought.'

As the last forkful went reluctantly into his mouth, she whisked the plate away.

'There,' she said, triumphantly. 'you do feel better, don't you? Fit enough to tell me what's got you into this state.'

Apart from his engine-room head, Ted did at least appreciate that the furniture had ceased hurtling round the room. He related the morning's happenings.

'I thought you were taking a risk when you first told me about that girl, but you're so conscientious, giving your time to slags like her who aren't capable, and never will be.'

'She is capable,' he said, stubbornly.

'Yeah, capable of losing you your job.'

'But I haven't done anything wrong.'

'There's no smoke without fire, that's what they'll be saying.'

'Well, thanks for your support.' But the dreadful knotting in his stomach told him she was right.

The phone rang.

'I'll get it.' Catherine went into the dining room and he heard her muffled voice and a conversation that seemed to go on for some time.

'That was Richard,' she said on her return. 'He said the news of your suspension spread round the school like nobody's business. Evidently the staff couldn't believe it and Richard was told by several of your pupils that all your classes are signing petitions. It was a good thing Little Miss Cromer wasn't in school, because she'd likely be lynched. And if it's all right, he and Sheila would like to come round tomorrow evening.'

The thought of his little seventh years getting up a petition caused a lump in his throat and he had to wipe away a maudlin tear.

When they were in bed, Ted said, 'I've missed you so much. Why haven't you come round? It's been nearly a month.'

'I haven't been well,' she said.

Ted sat up quickly, and regrettably given the circumstances, and rested on one elbow.

'Why didn't you tell me? What's wrong? Is it serious?'

Catherine shut her book and put it on the bedside table. 'The doctor sent me to the hospital; he thinks it's probably an ulcer.'

'Where?'

'In the stomach.'

'What sent you to him in the first place?'

'I'm off my food and when I do eat I feel sick.'

'What did they do?'

'Examined me, took an X-ray and said they'd get back.'

'If you'd said, I could have come with you.'

'What could you have done? I was all right.'

'I've missed you. I wished you loved me as much as I love you,' Ted said.

'What makes you think I don't love you?'

'I didn't say you didn't, but you won't marry me for a start.'

'You would take that as proof of my love, would you?'

'Isn't that what marriage is all about?'

'Why are there so many divorces then?'

'You know what I mean.'

'All right, I'll marry you.'

Ted gazed into the hazel eyes he so admired. 'Do you mean that?'

'I've just said so, haven't I? What do you want me to do, go and get a vicar now?'

'Oh, my darling.' Ted hugged her and smothered her face with kisses, though every movement sent the pistons moving.

'Did you find out where my daughter went?' she asked when she'd had enough of being kissed.

'Not where she went when she left here, but Denise, very reluctantly, gave me her office number, so I found out she was all right. I've written to her there, but she hasn't answered.'

'Well I found out she went to Denise's in the middle of the night. I bet Sylvia Gannon wasn't too pleased about that. The next couple of weeks she was with my mother.'

'I thought she was lying when she said she hadn't seen Lucy.'

'Evidently she swore my mother to secrecy, but even she doesn't know where Lucy's living now, inconsiderate little madam.'

'How can you say that? Lucy's had a rotten time.'

'Mother told her her father might still be alive.'

'I wish I'd told her that a long time ago. Now I've lost her.'

Ted sighed, remembering the good times they'd had, and how miserable and upset she was now.

'Not much of a loss if she can't be bothered to answer your letter.'

'Did your mother say anything else?'

'Like what?'

'If she was – getting over Ian – coming to terms with hearing about her father, you know.'

'No, she didn't.'

Ted lay back staring at the ceiling, concerned about Lucy – concerned and fearful. The fact that she had no father had always assumed major importance in Lucy's life, more so than with other children he'd known in that position. Poor Lucy, intelligent, kindly and unsophisticated, but capable of making big decisions as she had when she moved in with Ian. For all his shallowness, Ian had been a nice enough lad. Next time. Lucy might be hurt even more in her pursuit of love. The thought of someone not caring for her made Ted want to cry.

'You've gone very quiet,' Catherine said.

'I was thinking about Lucy.'

'I don't want you making love to me while you're thinking about her.'

'I wasn't intending to make love to you.' He grinned. 'I've still got a headache.'

*

'I shall stay at my flat tonight,' Catherine said two days later as they ate breakfast.

'Please don't, I need you here more than ever, can't you see?' he pleaded.

'I'll be back soon I promise. Nothing's going to happen today, is it?'

'But I want your support.'

In spite of Catherine's torture which had helped relieve him of his hangover, Ted still felt low, not to mention angry about his classes.

'I've got to do something,' she said.

'What?'

'It's private.'

'If we're going to get married, you shouldn't have private

things that I don't know about.'

'Well, I have,' she said sharply. She got up from the table and tipped her hand to reveal her watch. 'I'm late. I'll give you a ring when I'm coming back.' She gave Ted a kiss, and left him wondering if marriage to Catherine was what he wanted after all.

CHAPTER 5

'I can't stick it in 'ere any longer. I'm going for a walk.'

'Good idea, you need a bit of fresh air,' Lorraine's mother said as she put her carrier bags on the worktop and started unloading. 'You could stroll round the shops. You might see some of your friends.'

'I don't think they'll want to talk to me 'cause of what I've done.'

'He 'ad to be stopped, like what your Dad said, him in charge of young people an' all. I mean, he could...'

But Lorraine didn't stop to listen. She fetched her coat and furtively turning her head to peer left and right, she scuttled across the square and walked into the main road. Outside McDonald's she hovered and glanced in. At least six from her year were there, as well as others from lower down the school. She hurried past, head down, till she reached the park. She went through the open, gold-tipped wrought iron gates, and walked round the pond.

Lorraine had never been so miserable. She couldn't get Mr Lassiter out of her mind and was distraught over what she'd done. If she hadn't been so sulky and bad-tempered over the holiday, her father would not have lost his cool, and she would not have made up that story.

When Lorraine heard John was leaving and she would have him all to herself, she could hardly wait for the next term to begin. Then came Mr Lassiter's bombshell and all she could think about was getting her own back. Like a large stone rolling down hill, matters had gathered momentum. By the time she realised things were out of control, she seemed powerless to stop them.

'Look 'ere,' her father had said, 'I've 'ad enough of this. You're behaving more like what you did when you was fifteen. What's the matter with you? If schoolwork's too much, then leave. Me and your Mum never forced you to stay.'

'It's – it's Mr Lassiter. He don't want to give me them extra lessons next term.'

'Why's that then?'

'I don't know,' she lied.

Her mother studied Lorraine's face. 'There's somefin' else, ain't there?'

'Come on, out wiv it?' her father demanded.

'He, er, touched my hand.'

Her father's face began to colour but her mother chipped in quickly. 'Look, touching your hand ain't nothing, he was reassuring you.'

But Mr Cromer would not let the matter rest. 'What else did he do? You wouldn't be upset over a thing like that.'

How Lorraine wished she'd kept her mouth shut, that her desires had remained wishful thinking? She could have laughed it off, talked her father round.

'I'm going to write to the 'eadmaster and go up there.'

'No, Dad, please. Don't do that. Please.'

'But he's in charge of young children. There's no knowing what he'll get up to, or has already and ain't been found out.'

'He didn't mean anything.'

Her father would have none of it. He wrote to the school repeating what his daughter had said, and informing them she would not be returning. Nothing would have persuaded her to set foot in the place ever again. She knew how much he was admired. One of her year had phoned and told her he'd been suspended and all his classes were up in arms, and it would be a good idea if she stayed out of sight. What could she do? She was too scared to admit she'd made it all up.

Lorraine stood at the edge of the water and watched the ducks as they swam expectantly towards her, then she turned and walked over to a bench. She sat down and with her finger traced the initials already carved there. Then she traced an imaginary Lorraine loves Mr L....'

'You're Lorraine Cromer, aren't you?' a voice said.

Her head shot up, startled. 'Who are you?'

Catherine sat beside her. 'Never mind who I am, but I certainly know you.'

'What d'you want?' Lorraine stared at the woman, at the soft auburn hair, elegantly piled on her head. Recognition made her lower her eyes. She had seen her at school concerts. 'You're Mr Lassiter's friend,' she said falteringly.

'You've been lying and causing trouble, you vindictive little bitch.'

'How d'you know I'm not telling the truth?' she said defiantly, stung by the insult.

'Because I know Mr Lassiter and so do you. I know him better than he knows himself. His love of teaching is so intense, he doesn't see little mischief-makers like you trying to ruin his life.'

Lorraine's face crumpled. 'I didn't mean for Mr Lassiter to be suspended. My father jumped to conclusions.'

'Without you saying something? I don't think so. You do realise he'll lose his job and even if it is proved he did nothing wrong, it might be difficult for him to get another one, or promotion, because mud sticks. So, not only will you have ruined his life, you'll have deprived hundreds of children of a devoted teacher.'

Lorraine started to cry. 'He won't really lose his job, will he?'

'Of course he will, you stupid child. He's always taking ugly ducklings and trying to turn them into swans. You're the latest, only he was too kind to tell you where to get off. He knew what you were up to, but he still wanted to do his best for you.'

'I didn't think.' She sniffed and wiped her eyes with the back of her hand.

'That's the trouble, kids like you don't think.'

Without warning, Catherine let out a cry, clutched her stomach and doubled over. Alarmed, Lorraine stared at the woman. 'What's wrong?'

'Nothing.' Slowly Catherine straightened.

'You sure you're all right?'

'Yes.' She drew in a deep breath. 'Now go home and tell your parents exactly what happened. And if you think your courage might fail, think about the harm you've already done to someone even you might admire. I have contacts at St Jude's, so I'll know what's happening.'

Catherine stood up. 'Look at me,' she demanded as she regarded Lorraine. The frightened girl raised her head and the woman's eyes bored into her. 'If I hear you've not made a wholly and convincing retraction of what you alleged, I shall make sure your life is even worse than it is now.'

Catherine walked, with unhurried steps, through the park gates and disappeared from sight.

*

One evening, a letter from Denise awaited Lucy, asking if she would meet her as she had some news about Ted. Lucy wondered why Denise hadn't put it in the letter. What could be of such importance she needed to tell her? Denise had already told Ted where she worked, having forgotten Lucy didn't want anything more to do with him.

'Guess what?' Lucy said, when they had found a seat in the little café they used to frequent as youngsters.

'What?'

'After I got home that morning, who should come round later but Peter Evans.'

'What on earth did he want?'

'He said he'd help me look for my father. Not only that,' Lucy went on, pretending not to see the expression on Denise's face, 'I'm going out with him.'

'I hope you know what you're doing. It doesn't seem as if you take much notice of what I say.'

'Be happy for me, Denise. He's teaching me to drive and next time he goes away on business - he owns his own factory,' she added importantly, 'he's asked me if I'd like to go with him.'

Her friend did not look happy. 'I wash my hands of you. One minute the world has come to an end, the next you've flung yourself into another man's arms. And he is much older than you are. Where's that going to end I wonder?'

'It's not like that,' Lucy said, annoyed that Denise didn't share her delight.

'Where have I heard that before? I suppose he's got you into bed?'

'That's where you're wrong 'cause he hasn't.'

Lucy didn't want Peter to be that sort of person, but she wouldn't have minded a more romantic approach. Doubts that she had not entertained since she'd known him now crept unwillingly into her mind. Suppose she wasn't attractive enough for him? He had plenty of money and prospects and could have any girl he wanted. And, as Denise pointed out, he was quite a bit older than she was. Not wishing to dwell on this any more, she said, 'What is it about Ted that's so important?'

'I've heard that he's been suspended from his school after allegations of molesting a pupil.'

Lucy stared at Denise unable to speak. At last she said, 'No, you must've got it wrong. Ted molesting someone, it's – it's laughable.'

'Laughable or not, that's what's happened.'

'How long ago?'

'Not sure.'

'Do you know anything else?'

'No, I don't live near the school, do I? It's only by chance I got to hear because somebody mentioned it to my mother.'

Lucy knew enough about the inner workings of school to realise how serious this could be. 'He'll be suspended,' she said dully.

'Yes, that's what I said.'

'There's usually a Governors' meeting or something like that. This is terrible.'

'I thought you didn't care about him.'

'What shall I do? Shall I ring or write?' Lucy asked, wringing her hands with indecision.

'Peter will no doubt tell you,' Denise said, coldly. 'My advice wouldn't be good enough, even if I did feel like giving it.'

It was the most uncomfortable meal Lucy had ever eaten. She could not recall ever quarrelling with Denise. She had been Lucy's rock since the day they first started school together, her lifeline in the intimidating world with which she was only just coming to terms. They parted with a cool goodbye.

On the way back to her flat, Lucy went to a phone box. 'Hello Mum, it's Lucy. I've just heard about Ted.'

'Good of you to call. It's taken you long enough.'

'Denise has only just told me.'

'If you had any decency you'd have been in touch with me long before this and you'd have found out for yourself.'

'What happened exactly? It can't be true.'

'Are you really interested? You told Ted you never wanted to see him again.'

'Look Mum, if you don't want to speak to me, put me on to Ted.'

'He isn't in.' The phone went dead.

*

'I've rung all the Evans in the phone book who live in this area, but I've had no luck. Those who have a Peter in the family don't fit the bill. I asked one who sounded hopeful if he liked dancing, but he said he had two left feet, so no go there. The next thing we can do is go to St Catherine's House, see if we can find out anything there.' Peter leaped up. 'Let's go now.'

'They don't open on Saturdays.'

'Oh, well, never mind, let's go out anyway.'

He ran upstairs and was down in seconds, carrying Lucy's coat in one hand and his in the other.

'You take my breath away. Don't you ever walk?'

'No, life's too short. Come on.' He held out her coat and Lucy slipped her arms into it.

When they were in the car Peter said. 'Where shall we go?'

'A normal person would've decided that before now.'

'Are you implying, young lady, that I'm not normal?'

'Unusual then.'

'That's better. What about Hastings?'

When they had been travelling for some time Peter said, 'You're very quiet.'

'I'm worried about Ted. He didn't ring me back.'

'I thought you said you'd cut yourself off.'

It was one thing ignoring Ted because she was upset, but this was different. 'I - I don't like to think of him in trouble. It's very serious what he's been accused of, and I know it can't be true. I thought he might write to the office like he did before.'

'But you didn't answer. You can't have it both ways. Either you do or you don't want to keep in touch.'

'He wasn't in trouble then.'

They drove for some miles, Lucy's thoughts ranging over her childhood after her mother had met Ted, and the way he had been caring about her and stuck up for her when her mother was being particularly hateful.

'I've got to go to Dorchester next weekend,' Peter said.

'What?'

'I said, I'm going to Dorchester next weekend. Do you want to come?'

Lucy thought about Denise and her warnings. 'I don't know. I'm getting behind with my studies. I'm tired when I get home in the evenings, and I need the weekends to get a straight run at my books – not to mention a few household chores.'

'Look. Lucy,' Peter said, as they drew up at the lights, 'I don't know what you think of this suggestion, but I was wondering if you'd like a job at my factory?'

She laughed. 'You must be joking. I'm just getting away from a computer with the prospect of a career, so I'm not about to go into some dead-end job in a factory.'

'I wasn't thinking about computing. I want you to be something more important than that. I want you to learn about the company from the bottom, like I did.'

'But I know nothing about electrical components.'

'Neither did I. You don't have to know about making an object to sell it – well, only in a rudimentary way – you just need to know how the business is run, cash flow, that sort of thing. You've worked in a commercial office before,' he said, making it sound as if she'd been in middle management for ICI.

'I didn't have anything to do with the running of it. I more or less typed what was put in front of me.'

Peter let the matter rest till they were parked and walking along the promenade towards the Old Town.

'What I had in mind,' he continued eagerly, not to be put off by Lucy's supposed lack of experience, 'was for you to work in each department till you've learned about the inner workings and after that, you can help me get new business.' He smiled at her convinced there was nothing to it.

She frowned. 'I don't know. What does David Willman say?'

'I haven't discussed it with David. Anyway, I make the decisions. We've been thinking about getting a graduate trainee for some time. I'd rather have someone I know.'

'But I haven't got a degree.'

'Only because you never had the chance. Look, if I can learn on the job, so can you. Think about it and tell me later in the week.'

'I can't make such a decision in a couple of minutes – be realistic. If I give up my job at Trumper's, I might never get another chance of training in the legal profession. And another thing, I don't want to spend all my days at a keyboard. I told you.'

'But this will be the chance of a lifetime. You'll have a stake in the company.'

Lucy didn't see how. All she could see was a mass of problems. 'What about your mother? Didn't you say she had shares? Hasn't she got a say in all this?'

'I can handle my mother, and David come to that.' Peter put his arm round her waist, pulled her close and kissed her cheek. 'Say you'll consider it.'

*

Eleanor Evans stood at the bow window of her elegant flat overlooking the common in Tunbridge Wells. Her high-necked blouse and ramrod back reminded David Willman of an Edwardian lady about to admonish one of her servants.

'What do we know about this girl?' she asked.

'Not a lot. I was introduced to her when Peter brought her into the office one day, and whisked her round the factory. When they came back, we had tea and then he put her in a taxi for home.'

'And home? Where's that?'

'A bedsit in Lewisham.'

Eleanor looked down her nose. 'Anything else?'

'She's twenty-one, a redhead, nice-looking, about five feet four.'

'I meant her character,' she said testily.

Just as well he hadn't mentioned she had good legs. 'Not a great deal to go on. Peter left her alone with me for about ten minutes and I was impressed by the questions she asked. She's obviously quick on the uptake. On the other hand, she was very nervous.'

'I don't like it; I don't like it at all. Ever since he ran away from school, I've never had a moment's peace wondering what he's going to do next. Fancy hearing from your son that he was on a boat bound for India and we were not to worry. At seventeen!'

David remembered. The call in the early morning saying Peter was missing. Boys and police scouring the grounds of Dulwich College; Jack questioning the Headmaster about bullying, exam worries or anything that could have caused his disappearance, but no one could think of anything.

'He's calmed down now, Eleanor.'

She went to the grand piano and picked up a silver-framed photograph and studied it closely. 'He doesn't look much like Jack, apart from the crooked smile.'

'And charm,' David added.

'But where does Peter get this impetuous streak?'

'That impetuous streak got him back when Jack died. He could have refused.' He noticed her shoulders droop as she replaced the photo.

'I'll get Peter to bring her down here then I can see for myself. Lucy Daniels you say her name is? Ring through her telephone number when you get back.'

'She's not on the phone.'

'Her address then. I'll send her a personal invitation.'

Poor girl, David thought. If Lucy were nervous of him, she'd be petrified of Eleanor Evans.

*

Ted picked up the post from the mat. Sorting through the envelopes he selected the one he was dreading. He slit it open with fingers that seemed too weak for the task.

> *Dear Mr Lassiter,*
> *You are requested to come to a meeting on*
> *Monday in the Headmaster's office. You*
> *will have an opportunity to reply to the*
> *allegations made against you. You are advised*
> *to have with you a colleague or your Union*
> *Representative.*

It was signed by Gregory Warren, Chairman of the Governors.

'Is that a letter saying it was all a big mistake?' Catherine asked, as Ted returned to the dining room and tossed the letter on the breakfast table.

'No such luck. It's about the meeting. It's a bit optimistic of you to think it'd all blow over. You're usually the pessimistic one.'

Catherine glowered at him.

Later that morning, Ted rang Hugh Griggs, the Union Rep, and apologised for the short notice. They arranged to meet in the school car park. Hugh got into Ted's car as he turned off the engine, asking him how he was. He told him he felt awful and kept wondering who they'd been talking to and what they might have said that would incriminate him.

'Who's making the enquiries?' Hugh asked.

'Alan Nightingale, the Deputy Head, I gather.'

'But surely you've had some feed-back from your colleagues.'

'Only Richard. He was with me when I was suspended and is my closest friend. He said nobody believed a word of it.'

'That's something positive. Just tell the truth. You won't have all the Governors there. Probably only three – four at the most – and the Area Personnel Manager.'

'I've met him. The Head sought his advice as soon as he had contact from the Cromers. God, I wish I'd never set eyes on that child. I'll tell you this, I'll never, never give extra lessons to anyone, no matter how deserving they seem.'

They stepped out of the car and Ted slammed his door and locked it. But he may never teach again. He had tried to push that thought to the back of his mind, telling himself that it wouldn't come to that. But now the moment had arrived, his doubts about proving his innocence weighed heavily.

'Don't let this cloud the future. I'm sure you'll be all right,' Hugh reassured him.

The bell will be going soon, Ted thought, glancing at his watch. He should be taking his bright seventh years now, and the next period a ninth year and later in the day.... He couldn't bear to think about his exam classes. Who was teaching them now? What about Malcolm, who had recently lost his mother? Was he being handled sympathetically?

The Head's room was bright, with early morning sunshine catching the corner of his desk. Ranged in front of it were six chairs on which the Governors and Stephen were sitting when they arrived. Ted and Hugh were invited to sit facing them. It reminded him of his interview twenty years previously. He thought he was nervous then, but this was ten times worse. Gregory Warren made the introductions, then cleared his throat.

'Now, Mr Lassiter, this is not a trial...

You could have fooled me, Ted thought.

'...It is an informal enquiry to get the background and find out if there is any truth in the allegation made against you. You have, of course, read the transcript of the meeting Alan Nightingale had with Mr and Mrs Cromer?'

'I told the Head originally, and I can tell you now, there was absolutely no basis for this. Not one of the allegations is true,' Ted informed them.

'Yes, but perhaps something had happened.'

'Not on my part.'

'Take us back as far as your first association with Lorraine Cromer.'

Ted took a deep breath and tried to keep his hands still and his voice steady.

'Lorraine was in my tutor group in the eleventh year and I also taught her English. She is not an academic child, but I encouraged her to do her best. In the end she took five GCSEs and got all of them with C grades and a B for English. She was thrilled with these results. I told her that she could get a good job now. Then she told me she'd decided to stay on.'

'Did she give a reason?'

'She said she'd heard I was going to take an 'A' level class.' I bet that will be misconstrued, Ted thought.

Mrs Chalcott, a governor for a long as Ted could remember,

asked, 'Didn't you think it strange she wanted to stay because you were going to teach 'A' level.'

'I thought it strange she wanted to stay at all. She'd always told me she wanted to leave and earn money.'

'But didn't you smell a rat?'

'A rat?' Ted repeated, perfectly aware of the implication.

'That she wanted to stay because of you.'

'She would have to do more than English if she stayed. There were further GCSEs she could take, or try for better grades in the ones she had or take another 'A' level. I wasn't the only one who would be teaching her.'

'Were you pleased she was staying on?' Philip Piper, a parent governor enquired.

'Yes, I like to encourage pupils to stretch themselves, but I did think she'd reached her level and that she would struggle as she is – was doing.'

'But you didn't discourage her?'

'No.'

'Why, if you thought she hadn't got it in her?' Trevor Hammett asked.

'It's never been my policy to discourage anyone who wants to learn. Anyway, I was no longer her Group Tutor. I told her to go to the meetings they have for those who want to stay on in the twelfth year.'

'What grade did you think this girl would get in English?' enquired Mrs Chalcott.

'If she worked hard she could've got a low grade pass.'

'So that was the reason for the extra lessons you gave her.'

'Yes, but not only that. I thought it would give her a good start, stop her getting bored. She would be more likely to ask me if she didn't understand rather than ask in class. I have – I had several very bright pupils and she might have felt intimidated. I offered to coach another boy also.'

'Was he another of your lame ducks?' Mrs Chalcott asked.

Supercilious cow. 'I knew nothing about him and I'd never taught him English. All I knew was that he was a reluctant pupil whose father wanted him to stay on. I offered him lessons in order to keep his interest, and hopefully stop him disturbing the rest of the class. One inattentive pupil can alter a whole class atmosphere, putting off even the most able.'

Graham Manser and Hugh nodded in agreement.

'So,' she continued, 'you decided to have the lessons after school. Wouldn't it have been better to have them during the day, in a free period for instance?'

'Yes, of course it would, but we couldn't find a period that coincided for all three of us.'

'So, why not have them on a one-to-one basis?'

'I have never done so, it is not advisable.'

'Because of the situation you are in now?' Mr Piper said.

'Exactly.'

'How come then you were alone with this girl?' Mrs Chalcott demanded.

'The first occasion…'

Her eyebrows shot up. 'First occasion?'

Ted carried on as if she hadn't spoken '…John didn't turn up. Lorraine said she thought she saw him going out of the gate. I didn't feel I could send her away; it wasn't her fault.'

'Was this against your better judgement in view of what you've said?'

'I don't think that came into it. She was there, so I got on with it.'

'But you must have realised she had a crush on you?'

'I thought she might, I'm not that naïve, but I kept the lesson very short, just going over an essay she had written, barely twenty minutes if I remember rightly and vowed I would never be alone with her.'

'You didn't think of terminating the lesson altogether?'

'No, apart from what I said before, she was doing well and I enjoyed teaching her.'

As soon as he uttered the words, he realised how they would be misinterpreted. He glanced at Mrs Chalcott, who looked smug and at Manser and Hugh, who were frowning. Gregory Warren looked through his papers and selected what looked like a hand-written letter which, Ted supposed, was from the Cromers.

'Tell us about the last lesson of term.'

'John Denny finally persuaded his father to let him leave, but he didn't come and tell me in advance. So, once again, I had Lorraine on her own. I had already decided before I knew John was leaving that I wasn't going to give her after-school tuition this term because I thought she'd reached a satisfactory level to cope by herself, and partly because of the situation.'

'What do you mean by situation,' Mrs Chalcott questioned.

'That I would have her on her own.'

'Or that you were getting too fond of her.'

Ted almost leapt out of his chair. 'I resent that remark, Mrs Chalcott. I don't think you have any right to make such an observation. I was asked here to put my side of the story, not to answer false allegations from you.'

The Chairman said, 'I think you should withdraw that remark. It was quite uncalled for.'

Delia Chalcott looked as chastened as a woman of her self-importance could muster and muttered a short sentence, the only word of which Ted caught was sorry.

'Now,' Gregory Warren asked, 'did you at any time put your arm round Lorraine, kiss the top of her head and say she was a beautiful girl, or squeeze her hand or rest your hand on her leg, on more than one occasion.'

'No, never, not on any occasion, nor did the idea occur to me. I had no attraction towards Lorraine, other than a desire to encourage her to do her best.'

'Did you ever make any contact with her physically?'

Ted thought of the time Lorraine had touched his hand and wondered whether his truthfulness extended that far. 'No.'

'Thank you, Mr Lassiter.' Gregory turned to Hugh. 'Is there anything you wish to say?'

'No, I think he has answered your questions thoroughly and truthfully. You must all realise how a man in his position is open to allegations of this kind.'

'Yes, of course we do.' Gregory turned to the Governors. 'Here are the results of the Deputy Head's investigations. He spoke to....'

There was a sudden movement behind them and Ted and Hugh turned to see Kate Doggett in the doorway.

'There's a call for you, Stephen.'

The Head frowned. 'I told you I wasn't to be disturbed.'

'I think you will find this important.'

'Oh, very well.' He excused himself and hurried out of the room. Mrs Chalcott glared after him.

'Where was I – ah, yes? The Deputy Head spoke to all staff on the school premises after school on the days in question.

'This is a statement from the caretaker saying that the door of the classroom was always open, even though the noise of the polisher must have been irritating. Here's another from the cleaner who said that whenever she passed, or came into the room, the pupil was always on the other side of the desk.' He picked up other typewritten sheets. 'These are from teachers who had come looking for Mr Lassiter, who said that they had never seen anything untoward, and one of them remembered the particular afternoon in question and Lorraine was sitting on the other side of the desk.' He removed his glasses. 'Mr Lassiter has been at St Jude's ever since he graduated and his record here is impeccable. He is a very competent and respected teacher.'

Gregory replaced his glasses and picked up a wodge of letters of varying sizes and held them high. 'But these, unsolicited I might say, have been received from present pupils who have been, or are being taught by Mr Lassiter. Some are from members of staff who do not necessarily know him well.

'Two are from pupils who have been left for some years. They say that if it were not for his teaching and encouragement, they wouldn't be where they are today.'

Ted had a lump in his throat so large, he thought he would choke and he couldn't stop his eyes filling with tears which, he fervently hoped, wouldn't roll down his face.

Stephen Holloway burst into the room. 'I'm so sorry to have left you, but there has been a development of the most – the most....' He searched for a suitable word. 'It's wonderful news.'

Ted and Hugh swivelled on their chairs and they all stared expectantly.

'I have just had Mr Cromer on the line very apologetic. He says Lorraine has confessed to having made up the story. He said he and his wife were dealing with her, and they will be writing to us in due course.'

There were smiles all round and they shook hands with Ted. Only Mrs Chalcott gave the appearance of tight-lipped disappointment as she proffered a reluctant hand.

When Catherine arrived at Ted's that evening and caught up on the details he hadn't had time to tell her over the phone, she asked, 'What did Mr Cromer actually say?'

'Stephen didn't elaborate, and I don't know if any of the others were given more information after we'd gone. To tell you the truth, I couldn't wait to leave. They're going to write to me.'

'Shall we go out tonight to celebrate?' Catherine queried.

'You know, it must have taken a lot for Lorraine to retract that story.'

'Oh, I don't know. She had a pretty strong character to make it up in the first place.'

'But she's only a teenager.'

Catherine nearly exploded. 'Here's a girl who almost ruined your life and you're still making excuses for her. Something made her see the error of her ways, just be thankful she did it in time.'

Ted gave her a sideways glance. Her face held a strange expression. Amazing, enigmatic Catherine – you never knew what she was thinking. One minute she exhibited overwhelming love, at others she was distant, even cold, part of her allure, he supposed.

CHAPTER 6

Lucy was wide-awake though the clock only showed five. She picked up the duvet, threw it on the bed and padded over to the sink. She made tea and toast and took them over to the table. Pulling back the curtains she saw an angry red-streaked sky and grey clouds, the slate roofs wet and shiny in the dawn light.

Lucy bit into her toast. Why couldn't her life be straightforward? Just as she thought she had settled into a job with good prospects, along comes Peter offering her heaven knows what. It sounded exciting, but she wasn't qualified for what he wanted. Neither could she imagine his mother or David Willman welcoming her with joy.

Lucy liked David and his old-world courtesy, but would he want some inexperienced girlfriend of Peter's muscling in on a firm he had built up with his father. Furthermore, there was Mrs Evans. Peter said she was all right once you got to know her, but Lucy found this less than reassuring; she had heard people say that about her mother.

Supposing she did join the firm and she was a failure, she would be stuck in a job she couldn't do and have blown her chances of being a legal executive. No other solicitor would take her on when they knew she had left a company that had treated her so well.

Then there was Ted. She didn't know what had happened to him because he hadn't phoned back. Would the enquiry go against him, even though she knew he couldn't possibly be guilty? Why hadn't he written like he had before? Would he say about her quandary? *"A bird in the hand is worth two in the bush"* or *"Thou strong seducer, opportunity."* A quotation for every situation, that was Ted.

She took her plate and mug to the sink, fetched her books and settled down for a couple of hours' study. So engrossed was she, she didn't take in the first light tap on the door. A more urgent knock made her start.

'I've run out of milk,' said the young man from the flat below.

'Could you let me have some?'

'I haven't much myself till I go out.' Lucy went to the tiny fridge and reached for the milk. 'There's enough here for a drink,' she said, shaking the carton, 'and a small bowl of cereal, I should think.'

'Sure you can spare it?'

Lucy nodded and smiled. 'I've had my breakfast.'

Later that afternoon there was another knock.

'The returned milk.' He held out a carton.

'But I only gave you a little.'

'Never mind, it helped me out of a spot. I had to go out in a hurry and I'm dreadful if I don't have something to eat first thing.'

'Not good for you either.'

'No, no, you're right.'

He hovered and Lucy didn't like to shut the door in his face.

'My name's Drew, short for Andrew. Yours is Lucy, isn't it? I like that name. I've seen it – on envelopes – downstairs – on the hall table.' The words shot out like bursts from a gun and the fingers of one hand clutched those of the other.

'Nice to meet you.' Lucy held out her hand which Drew stared at before grasping it with his own sweaty palm, pumping it up and down with vigour, then realising he was still holding it, he let go as if it were a hot plate. A flush rose up Drew's neck into his sandy hair as he took a deep breath.

'Would you come to the pictures with me – tonight?'

'Oh, er, well, I was planning to study....'

Lucy glanced at his face and could hardly bear the bleak expression she saw. How many times had she been in a similar situation; like the time Denise's parents asked if she would like to go on holiday with them. She was so excited she had run all the way home to tell her mother. But she had flatly refused and informed the Gannons it was because they were going to take her grandmother out for days. How she had cried. Lucy was ordered not to mention it to Ted, and she had to make up a story about why she was miserable that summer.

'That would be nice,' she said, smiling at Drew. 'What are you planning to see, not that it matters? I haven't been to the pictures for months. Last time was with....' She thought it kinder not to mention a former boyfriend.

Drew was speechless and when he'd gathered himself, he said goodbye and leaped down the stairs two at a time, only to rush up again before her door had closed, to say he would call for her at seven. Lucy had never met anyone more nervous than she was assuming, as most shy people do, that she was the only person in the whole world who was unsure of herself.

*

It was after seven the following Wednesday when Peter came to the flat carrying a large box.

'I couldn't stand that thing any longer, so I bought you another television.'

Annoyed, Lucy watched as he went over to the socket and pulled out the plug.

'But I told you I hardly watch TV and you're never here to see it.'

'Well, I've done it now. It was cheap 'cause it has a scratch down one side.'

Illogically, Lucy felt as irritated about having a reject as she did about having it at all.

Peter removed the white portable set from the box and placed on the floor. 'Your bell working?' he asked.

'You know it is, you've just rung it.'

'I came round Saturday but there was no answer.'

'I was out. I went to the pictures.'

'I thought you were going to study.'

'I thought you were away for the weekend.'

'I changed my mind.'

'So did I.'

Peter put the new television on the bedside table, pushed in the plug and switched on. Instead of a two minute warm up, the machine leapt into instant action. The Coronation Street actors appeared rigid instead of undulating like a room full of belly dancers.

'What film did you see?'

'Ladies in Lavender.'

'Did you go with Denise?'

'Why am I being quizzed like this? You know I haven't seen Denise for ages. If you must know, the chap downstairs asked me.'

Peter's brows drew together as he put the old set into the box.

'You'd better leave that here,' Lucy said. 'It isn't mine.'

'Who'd want a thing like that?'

'I've no idea, but it belongs to the flat.'

'My mother wants us to go and see her,' he said, as he shut the flaps.

'I know, I had a letter from her this morning. I suppose she wants to give me the once-over. What have you told her?'

'Are you going out again?'

'Peter! What on earth are you talking about?'

'Are you going out with him again – this person downstairs?'

'He hasn't asked me, but if he does, I will. He's only a kid.'

'That's rich, coming from a twenty-one year old.'

'What's got into you? Why are you here anyway? We never meet during the week. You could've given me the set at the weekend.'

Peter shoved the box under the table and gave it a kick.

'I don't want it there,' Lucy protested, 'I won't be able to get my feet under.'

'Where do you want it then?'

She looked round the poky room. 'See if it'll go in the bottom of the wardrobe.'

Peter dragged the box from under the table and manoeuvred it across the room with his foot. He opened one ill-fitting door and the other fell open and hit him in the face. Peter swore and Lucy giggled.

'Want to go out for a meal?'

'No, I've something in the oven.'

'Leave it. Have it another night.'

'Stop pushing me around and answer my question?'

'What was it?'

'What have you told your mother about taking me on at the firm?'

'Nothing yet, though she knows we want another admin person.'

'And David Willman?'

'Same. Whatever they say, I shall have the last word.'

'It doesn't fill me with overwhelming confidence knowing two of your board might be antagonistic towards me.'

'They'll come round,' he said with his usual irritating smugness.

If Peter thought she was going to be bullied into submission, he'd better think again. Enough of her life had been spent being intimidated and coerced into doing what her mother wanted.

Lucy went to the oven and took out the metal dish and tipped the cauliflower cheese and broccoli onto a plate. She made tea, took two cups and saucers from the cupboard and carried the tray and her meal to the table. Noticing Lucy glancing his way, Peter quickly returned his gaze to the TV as the Coronation Street music played and the credits rolled up the screen. A strained silence like a taut clothesline stretched between them. She poured the tea.

'Do you want your tea over there, or are you coming to the table?'

'What?'

'Stop sulking. I may be a young twenty-one, but you're behaving like a two-year old. You're puerile.' Lucy rather liked that word, so she repeated it.

She was feeling elated with her a newly acquired confidence. It had taken someone like Drew to give her the self-assurance she'd always sought and admired in others. Last Saturday had been such fun. Drew had hung on her every word and she saw in him all her own hang-ups - that anxiety about saying anything, but wanting to be witty and with-it. He had bought her a box of chocolates and she had let him hold her hand. Lucy had enjoyed the film, but she wasn't sure he had. Every time she glanced his way he was staring at her. When they arrived back he insisted on walking up to her floor. She could see the tussle going on in his head over whether he would kiss her or not. Courage forsook him and a peck on the cheek was all he managed. It was almost like watching a mirror image of herself. She grinned.

'What are you laughing at?' Peter said, as he moved to the table and picked up his cup.

'Just something that happened to me.'

'With the spotty kid downstairs, I suppose.'

'Yes, it was actually.'

'Did he kiss you?'

'Yes.' So what if she was stretching the truth? She stood up and went to take her plate to the draining board. Peter caught her hand as she went by.

'Did you enjoy it?'

'It was very pleasant,' she said.

He snatched the plate from her hand and the knife and fork clattered to the floor. The plate broke in half as he threw it on the table. Peter took her in his arms and put his hand behind her head and kissed her. Lucy fought for breath and pushed him away.

'What d'you think you're doing?' she cried.

'I don't want you to go out with him again.'

This was the first time Peter had made any romantic move towards her, though she knew it was jealousy and not sentiment that had motivated him. But Lucy had experienced the heady sensation of power and she wasn't going to lose it now.

'I'll think about it,' she said. 'Now are you going to clear up this mess?'

*

'You don't have to come with me. I was OK last time,' Catherine said.

'But I want to,' Ted insisted.

'It'll only be for the results. The letter said there might be a need for another examination, though I can't think why.'

'I don't care. You have to travel up to London and you might not feel well after they've – they've fiddled about with you. Anyway, if you're all right afterwards, we can go to a matinee.'

'That's not a bad idea,' Catherine said, brightening.

Ted was relieved. He was going to go with her whatever she said, but he would rather have her approval than not. It made life easier and he needed that after last term's trauma.

'I wish they'd hurry up,' Catherine said, tapping her foot as they sat in the hospital waiting room. 'If an appointment is for eleven-thirty, that's when you ought to be seen. I don't suppose the consultant turned up till well after the first appointment time, it's a quarter past twelve already.'

'Please don't get worked up.' Ted was afraid she would walk out, as he'd seen her do many a time in shops if she were not served immediately.

'Catherine Daniels,' a voice called.

'Ah, there you are. I'll go and get a coffee and come back here. See you later, darling. Hope all goes well.' He gave her a hug.

Ted collected his plastic cup, bought a chocolate bar and cleared the mess left by the previous occupants. As he sipped his coffee, he thought about Catherine and how unwell she was. When she thought he wasn't looking, he'd seen her clutch her stomach in pain. Most of the summer holiday she had stayed at his house, which was unusual since Lucy had started work.

He had been so caught up in the school and Catherine's health that Lucy had not occupied his mind as much as usual. Why hadn't she got in touch? Just a line, just a call to say she was all right? He understood he'd let her down and hurt her, but she must've got over that by how. Perhaps he would write to her office again. She wouldn't know about the school enquiry. He could write briefly, mention Catherine hadn't been well; tell her she'd agreed to marry him at last. He wondered what she'd think about that. Yes, he'd definitely write tonight. He drained his coffee and returned to the waiting area, anxious to hear what the consultant had to say.

Catherine's face, when he saw her, said it all.

*

They arrived in time for coffee, obviously not expected to be late as Lucy could smell it perking in the kitchen of Mrs Evans' flat.

Peter's mother presented her cheek to be kissed by him and Lucy's hand was held briefly. They were instructed to go into the drawing room where she joined them a few moments later. A tray holding delicate blue and gold china cups and saucers, and a plate of biscuits, was placed on a small antique table, and she returned to the kitchen for the pot. All was conducted in silence.

'How are you, Mother?'

'I'm well.' She handed Lucy her cup. 'Help yourself to cream and sugar.'

'Are you getting out and about?' Peter asked.

'I try to walk on the Common most days and I've joined a bridge club. Occasionally I go to the Assembly Hall. There's always something going on in a town like this.'

Lucy said, 'Peter tells me you still drive. Do you go down to the coast?'

'I'm not in my dotage yet, Miss Daniels.'

'I don't think she implied that,' Peter said and Lucy smiled, grateful for his defence.

Eleanor Evans picked up the plate of biscuits and pointed it in Lucy's direction. She took one and the plate was handed to her son.

'What are you up to, Peter?'

'What do you mean?'

'You told me you wanted someone to train for an administrative post. Is Miss Daniels your choice and, if so, what are her qualifications?'

'You don't believe in wasting time, do you Mother?'

'There I take after you. I want to know where I stand but, unlike you, I don't like being rushed into things.'

'I think Lucy will be a good person to train for the new post we're going to create. I want us to expand and I need someone to help me get new business. She's capable, quick to learn and would have gone to university had it not been for her mother.'

Lucy felt as if she had melted into the expensive wallpaper. Nervously she fingered her bracelet and glancing up saw that Peter's mother was frowning at her. She put her hands in her lap like a naughty child. Her newly acquired confidence seemed to have vanished.

Eleanor addressed Lucy. 'What has your mother to do with it?'

'She wanted me to go out to work to earn some money. My father died before I was...' So frequently had Lucy had to explain her circumstances that the words came out pat, like an off-repeated poem. 'We hadn't enough money...' Lucy swallowed as she thought of her father.

'Lucy doesn't have to be interviewed by you. She's upset because she's only recently discovered her father hadn't died before she was born as she'd been led to believe. In fact, that's how we met - but this has nothing to do with what I want. Lucy would be a great asset to the company. I know it.' His features softened and he gave his mother a radiant smile. 'Is that so very sinister?'

'David also wonders what's behind it all. Couldn't you have put him in the picture?'

'I thought you ought to be consulted first.' He gave his mother another disarming smile.

'And what about you, Miss Daniels? Do you think you are capable of running a thriving business my husband started in 1957? Jack had only £2000 and David Willman even less. Apart from a small hitch some years back, they worked very hard to get the company where it is today.'

She glared at Lucy regarding her, no doubt, as the hitch of the millennium.

'I haven't made any decision yet,' Lucy told her. 'I have personal considerations of my own. I also need to know what Mr Willman thinks.' Lucy glanced from one to the other. Mrs Evans seemed to find her remarks reassuring; Peter's expression was darkly brooding. The next hour was spent in stilted conversation with Lucy hardly daring to speak.

When they were getting into the car Peter said, 'What did you mean telling my mother you hadn't made up your mind? I thought you were keen.'

'Don't put words into my mouth. You know I haven't come

to a final decision.'

They drove for a while then when they were on the A21 near Sevenoaks Peter pulled into a lay-by.

'What are we stopping for?'

'I want to get this quite clear. Do you, or do you not, want to take up my offer? I won't make it again.' His hands grasping the steering wheel showed white knuckles.

'Will you stop bullying me,' she said angrily, turning to face him.

'I like to know what's what,' he said, trying to sound more conciliatory.

'So do I and I'm not going to make a decision in ten minutes that might affect my whole life.'

'Suppose I asked you to marry me, what would you say?'

'No.'

Taken aback by her quick, brusque reply, he asked, 'Why not?'

'If I'm not ready to change my working life on a whim of yours, I'm even less likely to decide on something I consider a lifelong commitment,' she scoffed. 'You don't mean it anyway.'

He switched on the engine and put it into gear. He looked into his mirror and accelerated into the road, saying, 'I always get my own way in the end, you know.'

After their brief stop they travelled without speaking. Lucy had glanced at him several times, but his features were closed.

'Do you want to come in?' she asked, as they drew up outside her front door.

'I want you to come back and stay the night like you usually do.'

'And I told you I have to study.'

'There's no need – you're going to work for me.'

'We've had this conversation.' Lucy stepped from the car, which was in the middle of the road as there were no spaces. She glanced up the street. 'You'd better get going, there's a car coming and you're blocking the way.'

Peter uttered what sounded like an oilrig expletive and she watched as he grated the BMW into gear and shot dangerously up the street. As she turned to go up to the front door, she saw the first floor curtains twitch.

Drew stood in the doorway as she reached his landing. He appeared even younger than his eighteen years. Peter was tall and broad with dark hair, whereas Drew was tall and skinny with straight fair hair and a pale skin. The two could not be more contrasting.

'Hello, Drew, not working today?'

'No. I suppose you wouldn't come out with me again?' he asked, his voice tentative.

'When?'

His face relaxed at not being turned down. 'Tonight? Or tomorrow,' he added quickly.

'Not this weekend, I'm sorry.'

'Is that your boyfriend with the BMW?'

'Sort of.'

'I don't stand much of a chance with competition like that.'

'Look, Drew, I don't mind going out with you occasionally, but I don't want you to get serious. I'm not wanting a relationship at the moment.' Not even with Peter she thought.

Lucy hoped this was letting Drew down lightly. She didn't want to be unkind, but life was complicated enough as it was, and she had a lot of thinking to do. Drew's face was a mixture of relief and disappointment as he said, 'I'll ask you again sometime then.'

'I'll look forward to it,' she said, as she went up to her floor.

Her room smelled stale and musty and she pulled up the sash window to let in a little air. She hated the room and wished she could find something better. Peter had hinted at a much higher salary if she joined him. Was that to lure her or did the post command it? A company car was also mentioned but she hadn't even put in for a test. There was still her father to trace. Peter had suggested a detective agency and when Lucy had protested she couldn't possibly afford one, he said he would pay for it. He hadn't mentioned it again. Her quest for information on her lost father wouldn't seem important to him, would it? That was something else worrying her. Peter was making her increasingly indebted to him. And that silly marriage proposal – what was that all about?

Lucy changed, tied her hair back and gathered her books and papers. She had been enjoying the reading and research and even Mr Constant had been helpful. She couldn't let Trumper's down now, they had been so good to her.

Two hours later Lucy laid down her pencil, arched her back and stretched her arms in the air. She made a sandwich, and while waiting for the kettle to boil, went to the wardrobe and pulled out a box of books. She removed them one by one and piled them on the carpet till she found the dictionary she wanted. As she opened it the words on the flyleaf leapt out at her.

To my dear Princess
Happy sixteenth birthday
Ted

She recalled that spring when exams were about to start. Ted keeping her calm, listening to her revision and softening the barbs from her mother. How horrible she had been to Ted just because he hadn't told her what he knew about her father. He said he didn't know much and Lucy was sure that was true. If Catherine had put pressure on him there wasn't much option.

Lucy searched for the word she wanted and a page fell open where a postcard had been tucked in. It was a scene of Snowdon. She had sent it to Ted from Wales where she had gone on her first ever school trip away from home. He had paid for her, her mother refusing to contribute anything. She turned it over. There was her childish handwriting and spelling.

Dear Ted
We are sleeping in a dormatory. It has
been raining all the time and I am not
very warm. I love you very much.
Lucy

On her return Ted had fetched a map and they had studied where she'd been. He had given her a geography lesson, though to her it had seemed like fun. Lucy's throat constricted and she felt the hot tears forming as she put her head down on her arms and cried. All the hurt and anguish of the last few months, and the uncertainty of the future, came to a head in this one nostalgic card she had sent ten years ago.

When her tears had dried, she pushed away her books, grabbed the note pad and began her letter. She told Ted about her job and what she was studying for. She gave a lurid description of the ghastly room and told him about Peter. She toyed with the idea of seeking his opinion about the job offer, but decided not to. Finally, she asked the outcome of the trouble at school and mentioned she had phoned. She read it through then added a PS – *I miss you.*

Lucy felt quite rejuvenated when she had finished and wrote a letter to Denise suggesting they meet. Returning from the pillar box after this purging of her soul, she knocked on Drew's door.

Four days later the post brought Ted's reply. Lucy recognised his neat handwriting and tore open the envelope eagerly. Inside was little more than a note. Thinking he had been more upset by her treatment than she'd imagined, she unfolded the sheet with some misgiving.

> *Lucy dear*
> *So pleased to hear your news, but you must*
> *forgive me for not replying in like vein. The*
> *fact is Catherine has been diagnosed with*
> *an inoperable growth in the stomach.*
> *I cannot begin to tell you how I feel. I need*
> *you Lucy. Please come over.*
>
> *Ted*

She read the note twice unable to believe what it said. Her mother ill – the woman who had dominated Lucy's life, dying! It could not be. Catherine was always blooming with health never compassionate towards anyone who was not as fit as she was. Many's the time Lucy had been left ill and alone with a childhood illness and told she'd soon get over it. She slumped into the chair. Poor Ted. Catherine was his life. How would he cope without her?

CHAPTER 7

'Come in Princess.' Ted kissed her. 'How are you? You look different, sort of more grown-up.'

'Fed up with waiting for buses, otherwise OK.'

'Catherine's in the living room. She knows you're coming.'

Her mother was sitting in an armchair with a rug over her knees. Her face was thin and drawn with dark rings under her eyes. Her once beautiful auburn hair hung lankly on her shoulders.

'How are you, Mum?' She kissed her cheek.

'Dying. Haven't you been told?' Lucy unbuttoned her coat and Ted took it into the hall. 'Can't you have any treatment?'

'It's spread too far. I can have chemo, but there's no point.'

'Oh, Mum.' Much as she resented her mother, never would she have wished such a terrible thing on her. What could she say?

'I bet Ted's mollycoddling you.'

Her mother's face softened slightly as she said, 'I think he's more distressed than I am. Still, you'll soon be shot of me.'

'Please, please don't say things like that. I know you never wanted me, but you're the only mother I've got.'

Catherine gave a contorted smile. 'So, you'll miss me, will you?'

What did she want Lucy to say – that she loved her, in spite of the way she was treated? Shall I ask her if she's sorry she made my life hell?

'Yes Mum, I'll miss you.'

Ted came into the room carrying a glass of water and a small brown bottle. He handed the water to Catherine and shook a tablet into her hand.

'Does Nana know you're ill?'

'We could hardly keep it a secret,' she said as she handed the glass back.

Ted said, 'I told her last week as soon as we knew. She'll be over later today and is going to stay here when I go back to school.'

'Can I do anything, Ted?'

'Stop talking about me as if I weren't here.' Her voice rose harsh and ugly, and she started to cough.

'There, there,' Ted said, as he tenderly put his arm round her. 'Lucy only wants to help.' He turned to Lucy. 'I really don't think there is anything. The nurses come in twice a day and she can go to the Hospice once or twice a week.'

'I don't want to go to a hospice with everyone dying about me.'

Catherine's fresh outburst almost set her coughing again. Was there nothing Lucy could say that would not be pounced upon? Her mother's presence, as usual, reduced her to her fearful, inarticulate self.

Lucy went out of the room and through to the garden. She could hear Marcie's boys next door playing and a lawnmower whirring in the distance. The grass badly needed cutting. She used to help Ted in the summer holidays, that blissful time when she had him all to herself. Tears welled in her eyes. How disloyal she was, but she could not, just could not, bring herself to have any deep affection for her mother.

Ted's steps sounded on the patio as he came up behind her and put his arms on her shoulders.

'No, don't turn round – not for a moment.' His voice cracked with emotion.

She could feel his body tremble as he moved his arms down to clasp her. They stood quite still; their personal grief wrapped each of them in a different cloak.

'How long has she got?'

'Two, three months.'

Lucy contemplated the trees that shielded the garden from the houses in the next road. The leaves of the robinia were changing from lime green to yellow, heralding the autumn. When autumn had turned to winter, her mother would be dead.

'What will you do?'

'When Catherine's gone? Who can tell? I live for the moment, I can't think that far ahead.'

'Shall I come again? I don't seem to have done much good.'

'Come for me, Lucy. Come during the week in the late evening when I've got her to bed. If she wants to see you, she'll say so.'

Lucy turned and buried her head in his sweater and cried – a little for her mother, a little for herself, but mostly for Ted.

Without daring to look at each other, they went in.

*

It was two weeks after the Tunbridge Wells visit before Peter called on Lucy. She had rung him twice in her lunch hour to be told by his secretary that he was too busy to speak to her. She'd had little time to contact him again. Several evenings were spent at Streatham, each visit more harrowing than the last as her mother deteriorated before her eyes.

Lucy made no comment other than 'hello' as she let him in and he followed her upstairs.

'Have you made your decision?' he demanded, as he sat in the chair tapping his fingers on the wooden arm.

'No, I haven't. I have been in no position to think about anything. My mother's dying.'

'Oh Lucy, I am so sorry. I had no idea,' he said, shocked and genuinely upset.

'Would it have made any difference if you had? You wanted to sulk, so you sulked. I could've been going to give you the answer you so desperately needed, but you wanted to show who's boss by not taking my calls.'

'I did have someone with me when you called.'

'You've had people with you before, but you've spared me two minutes. I've never kept you long.' She had known he hadn't had anyone with him from the way Emily spoke to her.

'It's because you're not on the phone,' he began.

'Rubbish.'

'I'll buy you a mobile,' he said, eyes brightening.

'I don't want a mobile and I don't want you to buy me anything.'

'Look, let's not quarrel.' He got up and went to put his arm round her, but she moved away. Peter shrugged and moved to a chair by the table.

'Have you something cooking in that silly oven of yours, or can I take you out?'

Coldly, she said, 'You can take me out, but don't lecture me, I'm not in the mood. Neither have I made any decision yet, so if you want to withdraw your offer, go ahead.'

Peter's car was parked two turnings away and when they reached it, two scruffy kids were standing ominously close.

'Clear off,' Peter shouted as he came up to them. They scuttled away, one making a two-fingered gesture and the other

64

mouthing an obscenity.

'I hardly knew such words existed when I was their age. I wish you'd move out of here. If I have to park much farther away, I might as well walk.'

'I can't find or afford anything better.'

'You could if ...'

'Peter!'

'Sorry.'

Over her salmon, Lucy explained what had happened during the last fortnight and how pitiable it was to see the effect it was having on Ted. Peter asked the result of the enquiry and what was happening when Ted went back to school.

'I don't know how he's going to manage. He was exhausted at the end of last term, and the school holiday hasn't been much of a rest. He should have been preparing, but I haven't seen one textbook or notes out in the dining room. All he wants to do is talk when I'm there.' Lucy could picture his face and the abject misery she saw there.

'What about?'

'Catherine – just Catherine. How they met, what they'd done together, all of which I know. He told me she'd agreed to marry him at last, which just goes to make it all the more poignant. What's worst of all is he makes me feel so guilty. I can't feel about her like he does. I'm upset, of course I am, but....' Lucy put her knife and fork down and Peter reached out his hand to cover hers. 'It's Ted my tears are for. I can't bear it, I can't bear to see him suffering so.'

'Come back with me tonight. Get away from your awful place. You can relax and take your mind off things for a few hours. Tomorrow we could go for a walk or drive – whatever you like.' Peter looked at her expectantly.

The thought of being somewhere pleasant and tranquil was tempting, but how far could she trust Peter? 'It is going to be the same as usual, isn't it?'

'What d'you mean?'

'Since I was last at your house, you've kissed me in a fit of jealousy and made a ridiculous proposal of marriage, with absolutely no intimation you had any strong feelings for me. Just because you have made some sort of decision, don't assume I have.'

Peter stared at her, visibly shaken, 'Er, well, no Lucy. I don't want you to think....'

'That's good then.'

Lucy went to bed very early at Peter's and was asleep almost immediately. Next morning the smell of coffee wafted into her bedroom. She hurried downstairs. 'Why didn't you call me, it's gone nine.'

'I poked my head round the door, but you looked so peaceful, I left you. I was going to bring you breakfast in bed.'

Breakfast in bed! What a tempting thought. Lucy had never been indulged in such a manner. A little cosseting was what she could do with right now. Life didn't have to be so hard.

'If you don't mind me in my dressing down, I'll eat here.'

'I think you look lovely with your hair all tousled and your eyes still heavy with sleep.'

Was this part of Peter's softening-up process? Lucy threw him a warning glance.

'I can't help it, you do look sweet,' he said as he shot cereal into his bowl and pushed the box towards Lucy.

'I don't want cereal if we're going to have bacon and egg.' She went over to the cooker. 'I'll keep an eye on the pan.'

'Have you decided where you want to go?' he asked, spooning the last of the cornflakes into his mouth.

'I thought Leith Hill.' She frowned. 'Or was it Box Hill? Ted took us there once a long time ago. I seem to remember some sort of tower on the top.'

'Leith Hill it is then. If there's no tower there – I'll move it for you.'

All day they skirted round each other trying to think of non-controversial things to say. Peter was having the most difficulty because his life centred on the factory and he couldn't find a subject that didn't concern it in some form.

At last Lucy said, 'For heaven's sake, Peter, say what you want to say. I can't bear you to start another sentence and break off because you think I might bite your head off. Let's sit down here and you can get it off your chest.'

Peter spread out the tartan rug he had carried from the car. 'I can't get over you. You don't seem the same person you were when I first met you.'

'That idiotic creature who thought you were her father?' Lucy snorted with derision as she sat beside him. 'Come on, now you can tell me what you've been dying to say since yesterday.'

'I mentioned to David I wanted you in the firm.'

'And?'

'He's keen.' She raised a sceptical eyebrow. 'Well, he wasn't wholly against it,' he amended. 'He thought some of the men might not take kindly to a woman, they haven't been used to it.'

'But surely I wouldn't be in a position where I would be dealing with the men: that can be left to David and you. How many men are we talking about? I thought your workforce were all women.'

'There might be instructions to give to the foremen – when you've finished training, of course.'

'So you mean to tell me they can't take an instruction from a woman? How pathetic.'

'You're very young and they've been with us for twenty years or more.'

'I'll wear thick, brown stockings and horn-rimmed glasses. I could grow a moustache. They used to tell young officers in the army to do that, did you know?'

Peter grinned, sensing that Lucy was coming round to his way of thinking, as he knew she would. 'So, you haven't completely cast the idea out of your mind?'

'No, I told you I'd think about it. But I cannot make a final decision yet. Not until after the funeral.' She swallowed, still thinking of Ted and how lonely he would be without Catherine.

'I understand and I promise not to badger you.'

Though she would not admit it to Peter, and hardly acknowledged it to herself, it was the lure of the extra money to get her out of that room which was tipping her towards his offer. Going back to her place each evening was a nightmare. The hallway was dark as the bulb had gone. She had replaced it once, but one of the children in the ground floor flat had broken it and no one else bothered to replace it. Bikes and pushchairs lay dangerously across the foot of the stairs. The smell of food and the noise from the bottom flat was intolerable most of the time. Even though Peter had done some temporary repairs, the wiring was lethal. A decent flat, some smarter clothes and eventually a car were taking on a seductive allure she was finding hard to resist.

Lucy told Ted about Peter and his offer, hoping to have his advice, but he was only half listening and said if she thought it was a good idea, then she should go for it. Denise when she told her was not encouraging. She advised Lucy to be cautious and not to be rushed. She must consider what pitfalls there might be that

Peter hadn't foreseen, or was not choosing to tell her. Another consideration for Lucy was the fact that Peter was getting keen on her, but exactly what his intentions were, or how honourable, she was not so sure.

'It's funny thinking how naïve I used to be,' she told Denise. 'I thought when I left home my problems would be over, but I appear to have acquired new ones, and I have to make decisions I don't want to make.'

'It's called growing up,' Denise said sagely.

'I've done a great deal of that lately.'

*

When the new term started, Mrs Daniels moved into Ted's place. Lucy went over three evenings a week and it was good to talk to her grandmother. They reminisced about when she was little. If Ted were not sitting with Catherine, he would join in their conversation but then he would gaze into space, his lips would tremble and he would leave the room.

'I'm awfully worried about him, Nana. I haven't seen him doing any schoolwork. He doesn't seem able to concentrate.'

'You're not here all the time, dear. I have seen him marking a set of exercise books.'

It was as well that Ted had not been given an exam class. Probably the Department Head thought he would give him a break after last term's ordeal. Something that had cheered him up had been his GCSE results. All except eight of his class had passed above C grade.

At the beginning of October her mother was confined to bed permanently. Instead of the pale, haggard look Catherine once had, her face was highly coloured as if it were burning. The nurses said it would not be long and Ted protested that it was not even eight weeks, and they must be able to do something.

'Hush, Ted, hush,' Lucy said, her arms round him. 'You wouldn't want her to go on suffering like this, would you?'

'But I'll miss her so.'

Lucy stared at the small table covered with the detritus of the sick room – cotton wool, paper handkerchiefs, a jug of water and bottles of pills and painkillers. The air was thick with the indefinable smell of a sick room.

Ted asked for compassionate leave and sat beside Catherine hour after hour holding her hand, till Mrs Daniels would drag him away to eat. Lucy sat beside her mother's bed longing for her to say a word or make one gesture that indicated she might have loved her a little. The pain of years of rejection still ate into Lucy, smothering what she should have felt for her mother, but replacing it with guilt.

*

A black limousine drew up outside the crematorium. It was a cold, bright autumn Monday at the end of October. Lucy insisted that Ted and her grandmother should lead the small cortege. Peter, who had come in his own car, joined her to follow them. The wreath, of white chrysanthemums on the coffin, was from Ted and the card with it said, simply, *To my beloved.*

Catherine had no time for religion and would have been appalled at the address given by the vicar found for the occasion. There was one hymn and Ted read a poem by Christina Rosetti. Lucy did not know how he got through it. She had tears rolling down her cheeks, and Peter squeezed her hand tightly.

Among the mourners were a few colleagues from Catherine's office, Mrs Rix, who lived in the downstairs flat in Clapham, Richard and Sheila and Denise and her parents.

Lucy thought Ted remarkably composed as he stood outside the crematorium chapel. He had cried uncontrollably beside Catherine's bed after she'd died, till the nurse had to tell him that there were things she had to do. Though his eyes were red and swollen with weeping and his face ravaged by the emotion of the last two months, he was managing to smile and exchange a few words with everyone.

Only the Gannons, Peter, Sheila and Richard came back with the family. At the house Mrs Gates, Ted's cleaning lady, had set out a buffet in the dining room.

'It's so good to see you, Lucy,' Mrs Gates said. 'I ain't seen you for – for how long? You look quite the young lady.'

'Must be over a year. How are you and your family?'

'Not so bad considerin' and the rest of them's fine. I've got eleven grandchildren now y'know.'

'Really. Plenty to keep Ted in business for a few years then.'

'Don't 'e look bad?' They both glanced over to where Ted and Peter were talking. 'How's 'e gonna cope? He adored that woman, though I could never see it meself – oh, sorry, I was forgetting she was your mother.'

'I could never understand it either and I don't know what he'll do. You will keep an eye on him, and let me know if you think anything's wrong. I'll give you my address, I'm not on the phone.'

'Trouble is, luv, he's not around when I come in the week – not term time, no. Only 'olidays.' She paused. 'Tell you what though, I can come round one evening like, make some excuse 'bout leaving something behind.'

'That's marvellous. Now, I'd better go and talk to Denise and her parents. Thank you so much for what you've done today. Ted and I do appreciate it.'

'My pleasure, m'dear.' She patted Lucy's hand. 'That your young man over there? Looks nice. Going strong, are you?' She gave a wink.

'He seems to think so,' Lucy said, and with this remark which Mrs Gates took to mean yes, she went over to Denise.

Ted said to Peter, 'Lucy mentioned something about you offering her a job. Is that right?'

'I own a factory and we're wanting to expand the company. We were thinking of getting a graduate trainee and I think Lucy will fit the bill.'

'She's a very clever girl, you know.'

'Yes, I sussed that out. I think she would do well, even though she hasn't a degree.'

'Lucy would have got a degree standing on her head if it wasn't for…'

'Yes, she mentioned it,' Peter said hurriedly.

'She's told me about the room she's living in. It sounds very unsavoury. Can't you get her to move somewhere else?'

'I've tried, but she says she can't afford to move. If she works at my place her money would be so much more, and then she could rent something better. She won't make up her mind, and because of her mother has put her decision on hold. She can be very stubborn sometimes.'

'Yes, takes after her mother there. She could probably take over the tenancy of Catherine's flat. Has she thought of that?'

Peter's eyes lit up. 'She's not mentioned it.'

'Don't rush her. She's had one broken relationship and the news about her father upset her deeply. She has told you about it, hasn't she?'

'Yes, that's how we met. She thought I was….'

Lucy sidled up to them. 'What are you two talking about?'

'Ted said you could….' Peter began.

Ted put his fingers to his lips. 'Do you know Lucy's friend Denise. Go and talk to her while I have a few words with Lucy.'

Peter went off like a mildly reproved schoolboy. Ted put his arm round Lucy and guided her into the dining room where the remains of Mrs Gates' efforts were all but gone.

'Catherine didn't make a Will. You'll have to apply for Probate.'

'I don't want anything of hers.' Lucy said, forcefully. 'You can take it all.'

'I can't do that, Princess, I'm not her next of kin.'

'But you were going to get married.'

'But we didn't.' Ted blinked his eyes quickly. 'And the flat needs to be cleared, unless you choose to live there.'

'Live there?' Lucy's face held much the same expression as Peter's. 'I'd never thought of that. But the rent, I might not be able to afford it.'

'You'll have to get in touch with Mr Taggert. I'll pay till the end of the year, that'll give you time to tidy up Catherine's affairs.'

Lucy didn't want to tidy up her mother's affairs, but the thought of living back in Clapham caused her not a little excitement. At least she would have somewhere decent in which to do her entertaining.

'What do you think of Peter?' she asked.

'First impression good. He's keen for you to join his business.'

'I know.'

'But you're not leaping at the chance?'

'Not this time, Ted.'

'Sensible girl. Do you love him?'

'Not at the moment, perhaps when I know him better. He can be a bit bossy and I had enough of….' Better not to mention her mother.

'Well, I'd better go and see how Mrs Gates is getting on. She's been on her feet a long time.'

They walked into the hall. 'Ted? Catherine didn't say anything about my father, did she?'

He shook his head. 'No, Princess, I'm sorry. Your grandmother told me what she told you, and that was more than I knew.

Lucy had not wanted to ask that question but could not resist, even though she knew what the answer would be. How cruel her mother was, even in death.

CHAPTER 8

Lucy informed a delighted Peter that she would take up his offer, but she didn't want to start till after Christmas. He said that was ideal because it was the beginning of their financial year. He and David would plan a job specification and itinerary so Lucy would know what she was doing week by week.

Since her favourable decision, Peter's mood had changed. Gone was the I'll stamp-my-foot-if-I-don't-get-my-way, in its place all was self-satisfaction and bonhomie.

Lucy contacted the landlord about taking over the flat. Mr Taggert, who had known her since she and her mother had moved in, said he was delighted to think she would be living there again, but he did need to put up the rent because it was not economical. Lucy explained about the room she had in Lewisham and that she was thinking of changing her job, which would give her more money.

'Tell you what, I'll wait till you start in January. That nice Mr Lassiter has paid to the end of the year. Then we can come to some amicable arrangement. I'd rather have someone I know living there.'

'Oh, Mr Taggert, you are so kind.' She flung her arms round his neck and kissed him.

'Och, lassie,' he exclaimed, 'you used to kiss me like that when you were a wee girl. Do you remember?'

Lucy did. He always brought her sweets when he came to investigate some fault her mother had found. Lucy used to wish everything would go wrong, so he would come more often. They saw less of him when Ted came along because he dealt with any minor crises.

Though she did not have to clear the flat, she still had to dispose of her mother's belongings. Lucy asked Ted if he wanted the jewellery or other items he had bought Catherine, but he said he had enough memories in his head. If she didn't want anything, she was to deal with it as she thought fit. Lucy wanted to get rid of everything that reminded her of her mother. The clothes could go to Oxfam; nothing would fit her, even if she had wanted them.

*

'You've not been listening to a word I've said,' Peter remonstrated, as they sat over a celebratory dinner.

'I'm sorry, I was wishing I were tall and slim.'

'I like you just the way you are.'

Lucy was flattered. To be compared favourably with the leggy blondes he was used to was indeed gratifying, but she couldn't help feeling she was being soft-soaped, as her grandmother would say.

The waiter took their plates away and they ordered a dessert.

'Come and stay this weekend. You haven't stayed with me since your mother's funeral.'

'You see me part of most weekends. What difference does it make where we meet?'

'It's not the same.'

'I used to stay because I wanted to get away from that room.'

'Just a convenience, was I?' he said, pushing out his lips in a pout.

'You could say that.'

'I can't get over you; you appear to have altered, yet again, since your mother died.'

'It might have something to do with moving back into the flat. I thought I might feel uncomfortable there, that it would have too many unpleasant memories. There are those, but....' Lucy tried to put her feelings into words, '...but I can wander in and out of rooms, slam doors, break a cup, spill tea, make crumbs without having the world fall on my head. It was my home for eighteen years. There were some happy times.'

'What's that got to do with staying at my house?'

'I'm enjoying my independence and – I don't trust you.'

'What d'you mean by that?' he said indignantly, his dessert spoon poised halfway to his mouth.

'You know very well what I mean.'

'But you stayed with me when I was almost a complete stranger.'

'I know, and when I think back, I can't believe I was so incredibly stupid and naïve. Denise as good as told me so, but I didn't want to listen. In fact, when I first knew you, I wondered if something were wrong with me because you behaved so correctly.' Lucy smiled at him quizzically.

'I'm not a complete bastard. You were distressed and confused. You looked as if you needed protecting and I wanted to help you search for your father. Truly,' he added, in case she didn't believe him.

'And now?'

'I want you, but you no longer seem to want me.'

Lucy returned to her dessert.

'Well, aren't you going to say something?'

'You've got what you wanted – as you said you would. I shall be working for you.'

Peter looked smug. 'I always get what I want, even if I have to wait.'

Lucy changed the subject. 'I had a letter from Drew yesterday.

'Drew? Oh, him.'

'He said he missed me and that some horrible, middle-aged man in his early thirties had moved into my room.'

Peter grunted. 'He won't be taking him to the pictures then.' The penny dropped 'What d'you mean middle-aged man?'

Lucy giggled. 'He didn't say who was upstairs, but he has asked me out for a meal.'

'You're not going, of course.'

'I am going, of course. I treated him to a pizza when you were being churlish and wouldn't contact me. Now he's returning the invitation. Anyway, I like him, he makes me feel good.'

Peter's thick eyebrows drew together in the all too familiar frown of displeasure. 'Don't I?'

'Now, see here, Peter. If I'm going to work at your factory, don't you think it's going to make my life even more difficult if the rest of the workforce think I'm living with you?' Lucy let this sink in. 'Or, more likely, that I'm your current bit on the side.'

His frown deepened. 'You don't pull any punches, do you?'

'Do you?'

Peter spooned the last of his tiramasu into his mouth.

'Coffee?' he asked, as he carefully placed his spoon and fork side by side.

'That is how you see me, isn't it? A neat little package – business on the one hand combined with your sexual gratification on the other.'

'I wish you wouldn't speak like that.'

'But it's all right for you to think like that and what's more, assume I'm quite willing to fall in with your plans.'

74

Peter's face was like watching changing graphics on television. After the shock, embarrassment, then amusement as he grinned.

'I am a man after all.' He paused. 'You could marry me.'

'Peter, you don't love me and to marry me for sex is insulting.'

*

The first Monday in January saw Lucy up early and eager to start. She'd had a few misgivings in the middle of the night but, on the whole, she thought she was doing the right thing.

Mr Woodhead, the partner in Trumper's who had first encouraged Lucy to take exams, had been upset when she told him she was going to leave. In his gentlemanly way he wished her well. But Mr Constant told her she was a fool and that she had a bright future with them, and would she not reconsider before it was too late. It was about the longest sentence he had uttered other than for work.

Lucy had bought a dark green suit and shoes to match. In fact, she was newly attired from head to toe, having spent some of her mother's money. She was surprised Catherine had left as much as five thousand pounds, poverty being pleaded on every occasion Lucy wanted anything. She told Ted about the money and asked if he wanted it, but he said enjoy it. Having second thoughts about anything of her mother's, Lucy took great delight in spending what she considered should have been spent on her in the past.

Peter was eagerly awaiting her at the door. 'You look efficient and you've put your hair up again.'

'I thought it might make me appear older and it was easier than growing a moustache.'

'Come on, let's go and see David.' He put his arm round her and almost pushed her through the door.

David greeted her warmly and the three of them sat for an hour detailing where she was to be in the following weeks, and what she might expect from each department.

'First of all,' Peter said, 'when we've had a coffee, I'll take you round the offices and factory and introduce you properly. After lunch you can start in the Accounts Department.'

Peter was almost jumping up and down with excitement, much to her and David's amusement. When he went out of the office David said, 'That's Peter all over, when he's up - he's up.'

'And when he's down, he's a pest. I know, I've experienced it.'

'Are you feeling nervous?'

'A little, but not as much as I thought I would.'

Lucy had difficulty estimating what the reaction to her was. People had been polite in the offices, but on the factory floor most appeared disinterested, apart from the men who looked her up and down the way men do. She asked one or two questions of the girls who were stamping out or assembling parts, but they answered in monosyllables. According to her schedule, she was to work with them for a while later in the year.

After lunch she was ushered into Accounts. Gordon Ross reminded her of Mr Constant, a man of few words. When the firm had got off the ground, Peter told her, his father and David found they couldn't cope without more help, and Gordon Ross had joined them after a year.

'Sit over there.' Gordon Ross instructed, pointing to a small, old-fashioned wooden desk with three drawers down one side. 'Ask Lynne for any stationery you want.' He returned to his own desk and started working, leaving Lucy wondering what she was supposed to do next – with or without stationery.

She stowed her handbag in a drawer and went over to Lynne who was sitting in front of a computer. Lynne was in her early twenties with dyed blonde hair and a multitude of silver earrings along one ear.

'Can you tell me what you're doing?' Lucy asked.

'Invoices.'

'What else do you have to do besides those?'

'Sales orders.'

'Anything else?'

'End of year accounts.'

'Do you type any letters?'

'Only for Mr Ross. Emily does the interesting stuff?'

'Is that Peter's secretary'

'Yeah.'

'Do you spend all your time at the screen?'

'Yeah.' Lynne suddenly waxed eloquent. 'There's the filing.'

'How long have you been here?'

'Three years.'

'Do you like it?'

'S'all right.'

Lucy felt she had asked all she could without hindering Lynne and turned to Mr Ross. 'What do you want me to do? Can I help you, or look through files to get some background?'

'I'll be with you in a moment, Miss Daniels. Just sit there till I've finished what I'm doing.'

Lynne sniggered and Lucy's heart sank with this curt dismissal. Her stay in this department wasn't going to be a side-splitting adventure.

*

David leaned back in his chair in no hurry to go home. In the background he could hear the whirr of machinery; the second shift had another hour and a half to go. He started thinking about Lucy Daniels and this led to contemplating the company's beginning.

He had first met Jack Evans when they were in their late teens. They had not been close friends, but they saw each other every Saturday night. After Jack married Eleanor, they no longer had regular contact, but they did have a chance meeting a year later.

'Good Lord, fancy seeing you, Jack. How are you? And your wife?'

'We're fine David, and you?'

'OK thanks. Got married a few months ago.'

'I know, I got your card. I've been meaning to get in touch with you, but I lost your new address.'

David looked surprised. 'What for?'

'I'm thinking about setting up a factory and wondered whether you'd consider joining me.'

He was flabbergasted, not only at being asked, but the fact that it was to do with factory work, about which he knew absolutely nothing. 'Why me?'

'Because I like you, you're my type of person and I think we'd get on well.'

'What's your factory going to produce?' David asked, still unsettled by Jack's extraordinary proposal.

'Electrical components – plastic light fittings, plugs, that sort of thing.'

'But I don't know anything about – about that sort of thing.'

'Neither do I, but I'm sure we can find out as we go along. What do you think?' Jack asked, his eyes alight.

David had to admire his enthusiasm and went home to put it to his wife. With Bridget's reluctant agreement they had scraped together some money to put towards the venture. David was not in the same league financially as his friend, but Jack didn't seem to think it important and assured David that everything would turn out fine. Jack was the go-getter, the marketing man, while David concentrated on the personnel and factory side, and they learned as they went along. In addition, he tried to curb Jack's over-eagerness.

It was in the seventies that saw the only blip in their relationship. They began to experience difficulties with non-payment or late payment of bills. They, like other small businesses at the time, faced cash-flow problems. David, though worried, was optimistic and was sure they would overcome these difficulties if they cut their own salaries and lay off some workers till things improved. Jack, on the other hand, became more and more depressed. Eleanor, who herself was suffering after two miscarriages, was distraught as Jack took himself off for days without telling her.

'It's so out of character, David,' she said, when he had disappeared for a second time.

'Try not to worry,' he said, with more optimism than he felt. 'He'll be back to his usual self when things improve. It's been a shock and he can't see an end to it all. It's all doom and gloom as far as he's concerned.'

It was David's opinion that Jack was embarrassed by the situation and didn't want to burden his wife with his worries – though even he thought Jack's behaviour bizarre.

As predicted, when they eventually surfaced from their economic crisis, Jack emerged from his melancholy and threw himself into his work as he had when they first set out.

David turned his thoughts to Peter, so like his father in some respects. He was keen to expand and whilst David was not against it in theory, in practice he thought it too soon. The company was doing well, but expansion would mean finding larger premises and that was a costly business. Nor was he convinced Lucy was experienced enough for getting new orders. Intelligent and conscientious she may be, but it was still a man's world and he didn't think she had the toughness to force her opinions on reluctant customers, or thick-skinned enough to withstand the rebuffs. He had to admit, though, that he had noticed in the two months she'd been there, a more steely side to her than he had detected at their earlier meetings. He laughed out loud as he recalled Gordon Ross' face when Lynne was away, and Lucy polished off the invoices and sales orders in practically half the time it took Lynne. Gordon had not even known she could type.

He wondered how Peter was treating Lucy. When he was home from the rigs, Jack told him, he seemed to have a different girl lined up for as many weeks as he was home. Always tall, nearly always blonde and out for the good time he could give them. And that was the way he treated them – for a good time.

From the comments Peter made and what he had observed, Lucy Daniels didn't fit into any of Peter's categories and she certainly didn't give the impression she was in awe of him. Business was strictly business and nothing that passed between them could be misconstrued by any member of the company. Lucy wouldn't even let Peter drive her home, even though she had an awful two-bus journey.

David was not aware of all Peter was up to in his leisure time since he'd taken up the reins, but he was pretty sure girls had not loomed very large. Now the hard graft was over, he couldn't imagine him continuing his monastic life. Not with a girl like Lucy so handily placed.

*

By the middle of May, Lucy had completed her time in every area and today was her last on the assembly line. Strangely, she had found it the one she most enjoyed. It wasn't as if the work were interesting. In fact, it was deadly dull and repetitive, and she would glance at the clock and couldn't believe that only ten minutes had passed since she'd last looked at it. The impression on her first day in January had been way off the mark. The girls were great characters. Several were sole parents balancing home life and work with great cheerfulness. They were reticent at first till they discovered she had worked in a supermarket for a while, and that she was genuinely interested in their lives.

A particular favourite of hers was the aptly named Joy, a large buxom girl whose parents were from Jamaica. She had three children under seven and a husband who was out of work. Joy was one of six married women on the late shift because they had someone to look after the children till they got home. The extra money an hour they earned was valued, and made Lucy feel very humble. Peter told her she need not do the two till eight shift, but she insisted. Lucy wanted to meet everybody and experience what they had to experience.

It was tea break and she had bought cakes for them all to celebrate her birthday.

'Oh to be twenty-two again, eh girls?' Joy turned to another girl on the shift and dug her in the ribs.

'Hey, you, don't be too long on that break or I'll have

management on me.'

'She is management,' they chorused.

'Don't worry, Charlie, I'll make sure you don't get into trouble. I've got a cake for you too.'

He came over looking sheepish. 'Thank you, Miss Daniels.'

'Call me Lucy, all the others do.'

They returned to work, stopping only to giggle at the cream that had stuck to their noses.

*

Where've you been?' Peter asked, when she answered the phone.

'I've only just got in. I'm on the late shift, remember? And I don't have the benefit of a car.'

'I'd forgotten. You don't talk to me at work and I never know what you're doing.'

'Really?' she queried, finding it hard to believe.

'I wanted to make arrangements for your birthday tomorrow.'

'We celebrated with cream cakes this afternoon. Charlie Bennett was most concerned we didn't waste any time.'

'You're getting far too familiar with those girls.'

'Oh, don't be so stuffy. Now, are you going to pick me up or do you want to meet me somewhere?'

Peter's voice lightened. 'I'll come to you and we'll go up by underground. First we're going to a show and then for a romantic dinner.'

'How exciting. What time will you be here, fiveish?'

'Yeah, see you then.'

*

Peter pushed open Lucy's flat door, which she had left on the latch. She had asked Mrs Rix to let him in the front.

'I'm here, where are you?'

'Having a bath,' she called.

'Can I come and scrub your back?'

'No you may not.'

'Spoil sport. How d'you know I won't come and do it anyway.'

'Because I've locked the door.'

He was annoyed that she'd done that; had determined far enough ahead that he would arrive while she was still bathing. He thought of the many girls he had made love to and the wet, slippery feel of their bodies pressed to his after they'd showered. He wanted to tell her he could have any girl he wanted and what was so special about her. But he knew she would say he was quite free to go.

In the living room Lucy's birthday cards were neatly arranged round the ornaments and her hatpins on the mantelpiece. One was from Ted of kittens in a cardboard box, and another mildly funny referring to her age, was from Denise. Sylvia and Joe, he supposed, must be Denise's parents. Her grandmother's was a 'relation' card, which Peter had always thought naff. When he picked up the next large, gaudy card he was annoyed to find it was signed by everyone on the two shifts, Charlie Bennett and Bernie King included. He would have to have words with them. Peter's was next, large but not too flowery, with Happy Birthday the only printed words inside. Peter had taken ages deciding what to put. Finally he wrote

Lucy darling
Here's hoping you have
a lovely birthday
Love Peter

This reflected his sentiments for the evening. The last card he picked up he put down immediately when he saw the word Drew.

He heard the lock click and Lucy came into the living room in her bathrobe, rubbing her hair with a towel.

'Make yourself a cup of tea and one for me while I dry my hair. What shall I wear? Is it a very posh this place we're eating at?'

Peter's eyes slowly travelled down her body and up again. 'You're no safer in here than you were in the bathroom.'

'Ah, but I've got something on.'

'I could soon remedy that.'

'But you wouldn't, would you?'

Capitulating, and thinking about later that night, he said, 'No, I wouldn't, but you're driving me crazy. You hardly let me kiss you, and when you do I feel as if you're holding back.'

'I'm not wanting an affair, Peter. I've got to get more thick-skinned first. Then, when you're tired and stop feeling sorry for me, I can shrug my shoulders and put it down to experience.'

'I don't feel sorry for you at all,' he said miserably. 'It's me I feel sorry for.' His brows drew together like a concertina.

'Let's leave it at that then. Right,' Lucy went on, 'I've bought an emerald green dressy dress. Will that be all right for this restaurant you've chosen? Which of your girlfriends did you take there?'

Grumpily he said, 'None of them, I chose it especially for you.

When she had gone from the room he muttered, 'I always get what I want, and you're not going to be the exception.'

They laughed all the way home recalling the evening. They giggled hysterically about the woman who had fallen off her chair in the restaurant and couldn't get up because she had caught the heel of her shoe in her hem. And the small boy who had dropped some ice cream down a woman's neck in the theatre. They were still laughing when they reached Clapham Common where Peter went to the rank for a taxi.

'Might as well finish in style,' he said, as he put his arm round Lucy and started kissing her neck and fondling her breasts.

'I couldn't get over the sound system in the theatre. I thought my eardrums would burst.'

'Good though, wasn't it?' Peter said, his voice muffled as he kissed her ear lobe. 'My Dad liked Abba. He had a lot of their CDs.'

'Did he?' She tried to disentangle herself from his embrace. 'I think we drank too much wine. I have anyway.'

Peter smiled as he turned her face towards his and kissed her. For once she didn't tense up and responded with a fervour he had never encountered from her. He sensed his designs for the rest of the evening reaching a satisfactory conclusion.

'We're home,' she said, breaking away from him with difficulty.

When he came in from paying off the taxi, Lucy was curled up in the corner of the settee. Her shoes lay crazily halfway across the room where she had kicked them off. She was smiling sweetly and sleepily. Peter took off his jacket, loosened his tie and pushed her along so he could have her head resting on his shoulder.

'If you want a coffee, help yourself. I'm too tired to be a good hostess.'

'I don't want a coffee, I want to make love to you.'

'That's nice,' she said, and slid down so her head was on his lap.

'Can I?'

'There's plenty of coffee in the cupboard.' Lucy raised an arm and gestured languidly towards the kitchen.

'Lucy, don't go to sleep, it's late and I don't want to drive home to an empty house. I want to be with you, to stay the night.'

'That's nice.' Her eyes closed.

'Lucy! Why do you do this to me?' he cried, his voice

anguished.

Peter gazed at her sleeping face, at her light brown lashes and eyebrows, her fair skin with freckles across her nose. Peter thought he would die of love for her.

Love! He jerked so violently he woke her up.

'Wha'sa matter?'

'I hate to think.' He pulled her into a sitting position and kissed the top of her head. 'Let's get you to bed.'

Lucy let herself be led to her bedroom. The cold night air from the open window revived her. 'You're not going to....?'

'No, but I think you'd better take that dress off.'

When Peter had settled her, he sat holding her hand till she'd drifted off to sleep again. Never in all his life, he thought as he drank a glass of water, had he endured such self-control. He must be losing his touch. He left his glass in the sink, switched off the lights and went into the small room that had once been Lucy's. He took off his trousers and shirt and lay on the bare mattress, pulling a duvet over him. He tried to analyse his feelings, but the wine had had its effect on him also, and he was soon in a deep sleep.

He was dreaming. Stephanie was sitting on the bed kissing him. She was his favourite, quite happy to pick up where they had left off months previously. Peter knew there were plenty of men to fill the gap while he was away. She had more brain than most of the others and was sensational in bed.

Her face was close to his. She seemed so real he could feel her breath on his face. He opened his eyes and her hair enclosed them like a curtained cubicle. Peter put his arms around her and pulled her closer – so close she had to kiss him back.

'I see a good night's sleep hasn't dampened your desire.'

'Lucy! I thought you were – I thought I was dreaming.'

'Not about me obviously – how disappointing.'

When she drew away he saw she was dressed in jeans and a pink striped shirt.

'Let me get you some breakfast.' Lucy said. 'Are you washing first?'

Peter caught her hand. 'I'm going to kiss you first.'

Lucy let him pull her back on to the bed. 'While you pretend I'm the girl in your dream,' she said.

Peter let go her hand. 'You make everything sound so cynical.'

'That's rich, coming from you. I can remember enough about

last night to know what you had in mind. Unfortunately, you over-estimated the amount of wine needed to get me compliant.'

He tugged angrily at the duvet she was sitting on and swung his bare legs over the side of the bed. 'I'm going to wash.'

'I'm sorry, don't be cross with me. I had a wonderful time yesterday and I didn't thank you properly. Here's your kiss.'

She stood on tiptoe and he tried to look dispassionate, but she was so appealing he couldn't resist.

'Nice legs,' she called after him as he went out of the bedroom.

Peter sat at the breakfast table and pushed a black, oblong box towards her. 'I forgot to give you your present. You fell asleep on me. I was going to give it to you when we were in....' He felt his face flush.

If she noticed his hesitation she made no comment. Lucy took the box, opened it and found inside a string of pearls.

Her eyes lit up with delight. 'Oh, how lovely. I've never had a present like this. Put it on for me.' She came round the table and stood with her back to him.

'It doesn't go with jeans,' he said as he stood up.

'I don't care, I want to wear it right now.'

Peter fixed the clasp and planted a kiss on her neck. She turned round and returned his kiss, flinging her arms tight around him. If only she'd been like this last night.

'And before you ask if that's what I bought for my girlfriends, the answer's no.'

'I am horrid to you, aren't I?'

'Yes.' Was it worth trying his luck now? No, the moment had gone, and there was always his motto to comfort him.

CHAPTER 9

Ted boxed all the bottles he had rounded up and stowed them in a cupboard under the kitchen sink. He would take them to the recycling centre tomorrow, and then he would go to the shops.

What should he do now? Marking? Preparation? Didn't fancy it. Gardening? Lawn needed mowing, but it was too wet with dew. He could clear out some of Catherine's things, but he had no stomach for that either. He would just get himself a drink and sit in the garden.

Ted fetched a small wooden table and chair from the shed and collected a glass and bottle of whisky. He stared at it for a moment and made a mental note that it must go on his list. He was about to sit down when the doorbell went. Who the hell was that? Not another bloody neighbour who thought he couldn't cope?

'Good gracious, Lucy, what are you doing here on a weekday? I thought you were a hardworking business girl now.'

She walked into the living room and threw her coat into the chair. Just like Catherine did Ted thought with a stab.

'I'm skiving,' she said, as she sat down. 'I've taken a couple of hours off, especially as I knew it was half term and I wanted to thank you for my card and book token.'

'It was a bit uninspiring, Princess.'

'Not at all, you know how much I enjoy reading.'

'Well, tell me all your news. I haven't seen you for ages.'

'I didn't mean to neglect you, but I've been ever so busy. Peter likes his pound of flesh. Still, it is what I'm paid for.'

Lucy told him all she had done, describing the departments and the people who worked there. She made him smile over Gordon Ross, the dour Scot, who never said two words when one would do. She finished by regaling him with her birthday celebrations.

'Peter still keen on you?'

'Yes, but it's hard work keeping him at arm's length.'

'Does he want to marry you?'

'What he wants is an affair, it would spice up his life.'

'You know, you're getting so like Catherine.' Lucy pulled a face. 'You're more self-assured like she always was – as if you didn't need anyone.'

'I've always needed someone, but now I'm more wary and determined never to get hurt again, like I was by Ian and...'

Lucy stared at Ted. His face was flushed and he seemed different, but she couldn't fathom what was wrong. 'Are you all right, Ted? Are you eating properly?'

'Yes, of course,' he said shortly. 'Mrs Gates keeps asking me the same question. She was a pest after the funeral and was everlasting coming round on some flimsy pretext to see that I wasn't about to throw myself out of the window.'

'I'm sorry, that was my fault. I asked her to keep and eye on you. You look so much thinner. Are you really looking after yourself?' Lucy persisted.

'Marcie next door keeps sending me meals to put in the freezer. I must have about ten in there already.'

'They're meant to be eaten.'

'Don't fancy them.'

'So what do you eat?'

'For heaven's sake, stop nagging Lucy. I'm not starving.'

She looked him up and down. 'But you are a lot thinner. Come home and have dinner with me.'

'I don't want dinner with you,' he shouted. 'Leave me alone. I don't want to go to Catherine's flat, I'd see her everywhere, like I do here.'

'It's my flat now,' Lucy said defiantly.

Angry with each other, but neither feeling the need to apologise, they sat in silence for some minutes till Lucy said, 'I'd better get to work. I'm still relying on public transport. Not for long though, I've passed my test and I'm going to buy a car. I might even get a company car in a year or so.'

Ted handed Lucy her coat. 'Sorry I shouted at you.'

'Take care of yourself,' she said, as she kissed his cheek.

Lucy's bus drew up and she climbed on and walked to the front, sighing as she slid into the seat. She had seen less of Ted than she ought to have done since her mother had died and he was not coping as she thought he should. He seemed not to have come to terms with losing Catherine. How she wished she could give him some comfort, soothe him through the grief that was eating into him. Surely, after seven months, he could visit the flat.

*

David had finally been persuaded, or more likely coerced by Peter, into agreeing to move to larger premises. Lucy and Peter had been looking at prospective sites. Neither David nor Peter wanted to move out of London. Indeed, Peter wanted stay in the same area of south London. Today there was to be a meeting at Peter's house in Dulwich.

Lucy drove on to the drive behind Mrs Evans' car. As she stepped out, David drew into the kerb.

'Morning, Lucy.' He took his jacket and brief case from the car, zapped it and joined her. 'Like your car?'

'Wonderful, no more buses. But I'm still a bit nervous. I thought everything would be OK once I'd passed my test, but you're really still a learner – and the traffic's awful.'

They went into the dining room where David went over to Peter to speak with him. Lucy had been feeling confident till she saw Peter's mother already seated at the table. Involuntarily she felt for her bracelet. Mrs Evans glowered, making her feel she shouldn't be there at all which, as she was not on the board, was true. She fiddled with her cuff till she remembered she wasn't wearing a bracelet. Peter's mother was still scrutinising her and Lucy quickly put her hands by her sides.

'Did you, um, have a good journey?' Lucy said, as she sat beside her.

'The traffic seems to get worse and worse. You'd think that a Saturday morning would be relatively quiet, but there doesn't seem to be much difference. Just a few less lorries on the South Circular.'

'I know, I was telling David…'

'Right,' Peter said, anxious to start. 'Let's get going. Lucy?'

She reached into her case and handed Mrs Evans three sheets of paper with pictures and drawings. She glanced at Peter and David. 'I have spares here if you've forgotten yours.'

'I wouldn't dare,' David said laughing. He was always teasing her about her efficiency.

'We visited six sites,' Lucy began, and narrowed them to these three. The first is about a mile from our factory. It's older therefore cheaper, but it has the requisite amount of floor space to allow for further expansion and enough offices. The second is on a new industrial estate, much more expensive, but again has all that we require. The third has the larger factory floor area that we need, but the office part is not much bigger than at present and, as you know, we are pretty cramped.'

Peter said, 'I favour the new one. I know it's expensive, but with the extra business we get....'

'Wait a minute,' David interrupted, 'there's no guarantee we'll get this extra business. That's been my argument all along, and that's why I wanted to wait a bit longer till we have more capital behind us.'

'That's all very well, but which comes first,' Peter countered. 'If we don't get more business, we can't make more money, but if we do get more business and can't fulfil our orders, we'll lose that business and could even lose some of our regulars if we're not careful.'

'I think the older premises would be quite satisfactory,' Lucy said. 'We'd have to have it surveyed, but it looked well built. It has all we require and, when we are as successful as Peter thinks we're going to be, then we can move again, say in ten years time.'

'I thought it was an expensive business, moving? You surely wouldn't want to do it twice,' Eleanor said.

'No,' Peter said, 'that's why I favour the new premises, it allows for expansion.'

'We could be so successful that we have to move again anyway,' Lucy said, laughing.

'I admire your optimism, Miss Daniels, but we're not playing with monopoly money.'

Lucy was tempted to say 'Joke Mrs Evans' but let it go.

The arguments for and against the new and old premises raged till Peter's mother said she wanted a drink and it was time for a break. Lucy offered to make coffee, but Mrs Evans said she would do it and Peter would help, brooking no argument.

In the kitchen Eleanor said, 'You haven't done much to the house since I went. I reckon I could move back here and not feel as if I'd ever left.'

'I haven't had much time, have I?' Peter replied. 'It's taken all my energy to run the factory. Anyway, I need a wife before I start altering anything. Don't women like to beautify their own homes?'

'I suppose Miss Daniels is being lined up for the job?'

Peter arranged the cups on the tray without replying. Mrs Evans switched on the percolator.

'I thought when I first saw her, she was another of your floosies, but with more intelligence. From what I've seen and heard, she's not falling into your arms like all the others.'

'Floosies, Mother? That's an old-fashioned word.'

'Fits the bill, though.' She allowed herself a wry smile. 'I'm rather warming to the girl. It's time you were put in your place. You might be God's gift to women for a fling, but a wife is quite another matter.'

Lucy came into the kitchen and asked if she could take something in. Grinning, Peter handed her the tray and they followed with the coffee and biscuits.

By twelve thirty, with the pros and cons gone over several times, and Peter outnumbered two to one in favour of the older premises, Peter gave in magnanimously. Nevertheless, he was put out and Lucy could foresee some petulant days ahead.

'Let's go for lunch. I've ordered a meal at the hotel at the end of the Parade. We could walk there – give us a breath of fresh air.'

'Fresh air,' Mrs Evans exclaimed, wrinkling her nose. 'With those buses belching out fumes.'

'I expect you notice the difference,' Lucy said. 'I did, when I lived in the country and had to come into town every day.'

'I thought you lived with your mother in Clapham before you moved to Lewisham.'

Lucy felt her face flush at having to explain her circumstances yet again and glanced at Peter for help.

'Come on, Mother, I booked the table for one o'clock and it's nearly that now.'

He took her arm and ushered her through the front door and Lucy heard her saying that next time Peter was in the loft, would he get down the box of photographs, because she wanted to show some to her bridge club friends.

*

Lucy was to supervise the removal. It was arranged for a weekend in the middle of August. She had negotiated an excellent rate for the move and had confirmed all the arrangements in writing. Everything that could be packed in advance was neatly stacked and labelled. The building had been surveyed and inspected meticulously, the wiring had been checked and new points installed where necessary. To Peter's annoyance, David's amusement and their astonishment, she had taken the two foremen over the factory to get their opinions in case they thought of anything she had not covered.

'What did you want to do that for? It's nothing to do with

89

them,' Peter said.

'How can you say that? They spend a third of their day there. They could have good suggestions that we might not have thought about. Anyway, people like to be appreciated.'

'I suppose that's another dig at me.'

Lucy patted him on the arm. 'There, there, diddums.'

At eight on the Saturday morning of the removal, Lucy, David, Peter, Emily and Gordon Ross all stood in the car park of their new premises awaiting the arrival of the office equipment. Lucy decided it was better to have this arrive first, as anything that couldn't go through the front office entrance could go through the large factory one. Lucy didn't want heavy machinery and office removal people clashing with each other.

By eight forty-five Lucy was going hot and cold and everyone was staring at her.

'This is a fine state of affairs,' Peter said, scowling as only he could. 'Here we are standing around like lemons and nothing has arrived. You must have got the time wrong. Sure you've got the right day?'

'For the tenth time I've got the right day and the right time. I only confirmed it last night.'

'Well, something's wrong.' Peter marched up and down. 'I suppose they'll all arrive at the same time and that'll cause trouble. So much for your bright idea of staggering times.'

'Look here,' Lucy stormed at him, but at that moment a large van drove into the parking area, its offside light shattered.

'Thank God for that. Come on Emily, let's start telling them what goes where. You have been told which office is which, I presume?'

Eleven hours later Lucy collapsed into a chair in her very own office and Peter sat opposite.

'I'm shattered,' she said.

'Me too. Shall we go out and eat?'

'No, I'm too tired to eat. I want to go home, but I'm too knackered to do even that at the moment.'

'Poor old Lucy. You must be delighted with how everything has gone.'

'You weren't saying that earlier.'

'Sorry, you know what I'm like when I'm worked up.'

'Yes, I am pleased. I shall feel happier when we're all back to normal.

That's going to take some weeks.'

'Weeks!' he exploded.

'Yes, weeks. I expect the assembly line will get back on its feet pretty quickly, but the office staff will take longer. Files and disks get mislaid. Everyone's disorientated and won't be able to get down to what they normally do as routine.'

'Oh, well, the worst is over. Are you ready to go? Shall I follow you home?' Peter asked hopefully as they stood by her car.

'No, I wouldn't be much company. I'll see you tomorrow, about one.' She put the car into gear and drove off, Peter staring sadly after her.

*

Very upbeat after the successful move, Peter threw himself into acquiring new business. He sought out all his contacts for advice and drew up a list of promising companies he could visit. He told Lucy they would do three or four together, then she could go it alone.

After their first and second meetings with prospective customers, Lucy thought it was a doddle. True Peter had to work hard, exercising his charm at which he was adept, but small trial orders were given. They had a celebratory drink on the first occasion and returned home. On the second they were too far away and stayed the night.

'Single rooms are very expensive.' Peter said, eyeing her over his wineglass at dinner.

'Staying at a cheaper hotel would solve that,' Lucy replied. 'It doesn't have to be five star.'

'You've got an answer for everything.'

'And you never give up.' She held up her hand as he went to speak. 'Don't say it.'

He chuckled and her heart gave a little lift. She could see why women fell for him. He wasn't what you would call handsome, but he was nice-looking. She studied him more closely. His hair was thick, his eyes were the same blue as Ted's, the same as hers now she came to think of it. His mouth was well formed and nose a good shape. Yes, he was very attractive. Pity he wasn't the marrying kind.

'Why are you gazing at me like that?'

'It's not adoration, if that's what you're hoping.'

'I've ceased hoping for anything from you.'

'Wouldn't that be at odds with your motto?'

It was eleven-thirty when the Managing Director of Timetronics met them.

'Mr Crushin? I'm Peter Evans and this is my assistant, Lucy Daniels.'

Donald Crushin was in his late forties, short, portly and balding. He shook hands with them both, holding on to Lucy's longer than she felt was necessary.

He led them into his office which made the ones at the factory seem like broom cupboards. Two seats were already placed on the opposite side of his desk.

Whilst Peter began his rehearsed patter, Donald Crushin was staring at Lucy, not listening to a word Peter was saying. When he paused for a comment, Mr Crushin said, 'When your secretary phoned saying there were two of you coming, I didn't realise it was going to be a young lady – and such a pretty one at that.' He leered at Lucy.

'Miss Daniels is learning the ropes.'

'Is she now?' He winked at Peter, and Lucy wondered how he was going to react.

Peter smiled weakly and tried to get back his attention. 'Mr Crushin.'

'Mr Evans.'

'As I said, my firm is expanding and we were hoping you might be able to put work our way. I sent you draft proposals and the standing of my firm. Perhaps you would let us....'

'Yes, yes, I read them. Why don't we talk about this over a spot of lunch?'

Lucy could tell that Peter would rather talk in a quiet office than in a restaurant, but he was in his hands.

'Very well,' Peter said.

The *Horse and Groom* was a former coaching inn on the main road outside Basingstoke. Two steps went up from the street into the hotel. The restaurant was on the right, and a small bar on the left. As he passed the reception desk he said to the girl, 'Tracy, get someone to take our order, there's a love.' As Mr Crushin led them through to another less crowded room at the rear, Lucy detected an expression on the Receptionist's face similar to her own.

Peter sat in an armchair. Lucy, to her regret, sat in the corner of a settee where Mr Crushin now planted himself. He patted her knee.

'Now, how is it you've got mixed up in business negotiations? You should be at home looking decorative.'

'I'm very versatile,' she said, coolly. 'I can do both.'

He threw back his bald head and gave a loud guffaw. 'Got yourself a good one here.'

Lucy glanced at Peter who had a stupid grin on his face. 'It's strictly business. I'm a married man with four children.'

Lucy's eyes widened.

'No need to let that worry you.' Crushin exploded with another coarse laugh.

He did not let up all through lunch, twisting perfectly innocent remarks with innuendo. The last straw was when she felt the man's shoe brushing against her calf and his hand resting on her knee. Lucy tried to signal to Peter with her eyes, but he wasn't looking her way. She put her hand under the table and tapped Peter's leg. He beamed, and his hand sought hers and squeezed it. Dear heaven, she thought, what will he be reading into that. Eventually she could stand it no longer and said she must go to the Ladies.

'We'll see you in the same lounge where we had our drinks, my love,' he called after her. 'When you've made yourself beautiful – or should I say, more beautiful.'

Lucy tried to get Peter on his own, but Crushin stuck to her like press to a celebrity. It wasn't until they were back at the office that Peter managed to pin the man down. Perhaps that wasn't quite the phrase, but he did say he would look into Peter's proposition, and perhaps they could have another meeting sometime – and be sure to bring the little lady with him. Lucy thought she would be sick.

'Why didn't you do something about that odious man?' she stormed at Peter when they'd left.

'You made a big hit with him. Good for business.'

'I can't believe you said that.'

'Why are you getting so uptight? He was only flirting.'

'Flirting! Flirting I can understand. If someone like him can treat me like that with you there, what might happen when I'm on my own? You should have put him in his place.'

They had now reached their hotel. 'What did he do then that so upset you?'

'Apart from what you could see and hear for yourself, do you mean?' Lucy said, sarcastically. 'He was brushing his shoe up and down my leg and putting his hand on my knee. I tried to attract your attention to no avail. Then I thought of trying a more subtle approach – like kicking you on the shin. What with him groping me on one side and you getting ideas on the other, I felt like something on a market stall.'

'Sorry,' he smirked, 'I thought my luck was in.'

'I don't think it in the slightest bit funny and I don't think you're sorry either.' The rage in her grew. 'And I don't want to stay here tonight. I'll see you in the foyer at – at five.' She plucked the time out of the blue. To the Receptionist she said, 'Room 106, please.'

Peter tried to appear contrite, but only succeeded in grinning. 'What do you want to do then, eat here or on the way home? Or you could come to my place.'

Lucy became even angrier when she noticed the Receptionist looking from one to the other, with growing interest in the conversation.

'I don't go out with married men,' Lucy said very loudly, and stormed over to the lift. She hadn't seen Peter's face, but she had caught sight of the Receptionist who was having difficulty stifling a laugh.

CHAPTER 10

She almost didn't recognise him; his face had changed so much. Perhaps she shouldn't have come.

'Yes?' he said.

'Hello, Mr Lassiter.'

He screwed up his eyes and peered at her face. 'Lorraine?'

She nodded. 'I 'ad an awful job finding you. You're not in the telephone book.'

He went on staring. She hoped he didn't think she was out to make trouble? At last he said, 'Well, what do you want?'

'I want to tell you....'

'.... how sorry you were,' he finished. 'You did that in your letter.'

'No - I mean yes, of course I was sorry, but there's something else.'

'We can't talk on the doorstep,' he said sharply, 'you'd better come in.'

Lorraine followed him into the room at the front of the house. She watched as he cleared glasses and a bottle from the table by his chair and took them away. She stood where he'd left her.

'Sit down,' Ted said, when he returned. 'What is it you want to tell me?'

'I passed.'

'Passed?'

'I got my English - a B. You see,' she went on, 'I thought when I'd done such a terrible thing, the only way I could, like, make it up to you was to go on. So I went to evening classes. She weren't such a good teacher as you, but I worked 'ard, really 'ard, Mr Lassiter, I, like, tried to remember all what you taught us, and I learned everything by heart.'

'Everything?'

'Well, nearly. Most of the poems and all them big speeches in '*Anthony and Cleopatra*', like you said.'

Tears started at the back of his eyes. 'I don't know what to say.'

'Are you pleased, Sir?'

'Oh, Lorraine, you don't realise, you just don't realise how much.'

'How did our class do?'

'All passed A to D, except Tracey, Eric and Jackie.'

'And the clever dicks?'

Ted smiled. 'Eight As.'

'I always knew you was a good teacher, Mr Lassiter.'

He made no comment then said, 'I'm thinking of giving up.'

'Giving up!' she cried, appalled. 'Give up teaching! But you can't do that, you can't. You're one of the best teachers in the world. Your girlfriend said....'

'Girlfriend? Catherine? When did you meet her?'

Lorraine flushed. 'She followed me one day when I was 'ome – not at school I mean. She said I'd ruined your life and that lots of children wouldn't now have a good teacher. I wanted to do something about it, you know, like the trouble I'd caused, but I got myself in too deep and I didn't know what to do. I was frigh'ned what me Dad would do to me, but your girlfriend forced me to, you see.'

Ted's elbows rested on his knees and he raised his hands to cover his face.

'So it was after I'd written to you I thought the only way I could really, really show I was sorry was to go on with the English.'

Trickles of tears ran down between Ted's fingers and across the back of his hands.

'Mr Lassiter, you will tell her what I've done, won't you? She said kids like me didn't think, and I wanted to show she was wrong.'

His voice was muffled. 'It's too late, Lorraine. She died last year.'

'Oh, Sir.'

Sobs shook his shoulders and Lorraine wanted to go over and comfort him but remembering the trouble she had caused she didn't like to. She thought of her family's first reaction to any crisis.

'I'll get some tea, shall I?'

He was too overcome to reply, so she left the room to find the kitchen, hoping it would give him time to pull himself together.

'Do you feel better now?' she said, putting a tray down on the table. 'I brought a mug for myself. 'ope you don't mind.'

Lorraine hadn't been able to see any biscuits and didn't like to look in the cupboards. She did notice that the kitchen was full of glasses and dirty dishes that must have been there for days.

Mr Lassiter looked more composed as she handed him a mug. He spooned in sugar and slowly stirred his tea. She noticed his hands with their long fingers, which she used to admire. His thin wrists poked out from frayed cuffs as he tipped the mug. He pulled a face.

'Is it too strong, Sir. I didn't know how you liked it.'

'It's fine, thank you.'

They sat in silence for some time till she said at last. 'I thought I might teach. Do you think I'd be any good?'

'I don't know, Lorraine. Teaching isn't like it was when I started twenty odd years ago. There's more paper work, league tables, SATS, Ofsted visits.'

'But I wouldn't know no different, would I?'

'That's true, I suppose the essence of teaching is the same. I've lost it now, so I'm not the best person to advise you. You'd need more 'A' levels.'

'I was gonna sign on for history in the autumn, I didn't like the sociology I was doing at school.'

'It's going to take you a long time.'

'You think I'll lose interest and give up before I get there, don't you? But you said education was never lost. It wasn't just about taking exams, it was a – a – I've forgotten the word.'

'An entity in itself.'

'Yeah, yeah, that's right. Education is never wasted, you said.' She stared at his flushed face and thought how ill he looked. 'Mr Lassiter, is something wrong? You don't look very well and – and I couldn't help noticing all them dishes and things in the sink.' Perceptively she added, 'Is it 'cos you miss her?'

'I think you'd better go now.' Ted stood up and moved towards the hall. 'I am touched by what you did and very, very pleased for you.'

At the front door Lorraine said, 'Enjoy your summer holiday, Mr Lassiter.' She shut the gate and said over it, 'Please don't give up teaching. I'm sure things aren't as bad as you think.'

Ted shut the front door and went into the kitchen to rescue his bottle and glass. 'But they are, Lorraine. I'm afraid they are.'

*

Lucy glanced at the clock as she put the lid on the potatoes and lit the gas. She opened the oven and inspected the salmon filets; she checked the table, pointing at each item and muttering, 'knives, forks, spoons, serviettes, salt, pepper.' She bit the tip of her finger. Anything else? Water. She filled a glass jug and fetched glasses. All was under control and she stood back satisfied. Lucy did so want everything to be nice for him.

As she tidied her hair in the bathroom she noticed the dark circles under her eyes. Sleep had eluded her recently and the factory had been a nightmare this past week. The removal teething troubles were not over and she seemed to be bombarded from all sides to solve problems that were nothing to do with her, just because she'd arranged the move.

Since they'd returned from the hotel, Peter had been in a foul mood, sending messages via Emily so he could avoid speaking to her. Lucy thought he was being even more childish than usual. He ought to have had Catherine for a mother, that would have rubbed a few rough edges off him.

The journey back from Basingstoke had been uncomfortable right from the start. Peter had strode straight past her in the foyer, not even offering to take her case. He drove too fast, in silence, apart from swearing at every driver who crossed his path, literally as well as metaphorically. Peter dropped her outside her flat; told her he had opened the boot and left her to get her case. Lucy slammed the boot and went to say goodbye, but he sped off.

Thank goodness it was Friday. She was looking forward to a peaceful weekend, and this would be a pleasant start.

'Come in, Drew. It is lovely to see you.' He handed her a bunch of crimson chrysanthemums.

'Thank you, aren't they a lovely colour.' She gave him a kiss on the cheek. She noticed he had filled out and was less like the spotty kid of Peter's description, and more a young man.

'Come through to the kitchen. I haven't a dining room, but this is a bit better than the gruesome room at Tefley Road, don't you think?'

Filling a glass vase with water, she arranged the flowers. 'Have you found anywhere better?' she asked him.

'No, not yet, I'm still looking.'

'Dinner won't be a minute. What would you like to drink? Lager, gin, sherry? I've wine, red or white.'

'Lager please.'

Over the meal, Drew told her the supermarket manager had

suggested he try for a management course.

'I don't know what to do, Lucy. I'm so worried. I don't think I'd be very good.'

'You go for it, Drew. It might be hard to begin with and I don't suppose the money's very good, but you'll have training that will always stand you in good stead. It'll go on your CV even if you change career. They must think you're management material, otherwise they wouldn't have suggested it, would they?'

'Do you think so?' Drew beamed as if she had told him he'd won the lottery. 'You do make things so clear for me.'

Lucy thought having a mother like Catherine might have been better than having no relations at all, and she'd always had Ted and Nana to give her advice. Poor Drew, it must be daunting to have been brought up in a children's home, however well run.

'What's the matter?' Drew said, alarmed, as he scrutinised her frowning face. 'You do really think I can do it, don't you?'

'Of course I do. It was just that I was thinking of you having no relatives to talk to, and my father suddenly came to mind. I hadn't thought about him for ages. Do you remember I told you I was trying to trace him? I think we've pursued any likely avenue now.'

' I 'pect you've been busy in your new job?'

'You can say that again. I've been there nine months and have worked in every department. Now we've moved and I'm negotiating new business because the firm wants to expand.'

'You look –,'

'Yes?'

'You look tired.' Then added with a rush. 'But very beautiful.'

Lucy smiled. 'Thank you, you do do me good.' She cleared the plates and brought out a chocolate gateau and cream from the fridge.

Later in the other room, Lucy said. 'Tell me what else you've been doing?'

'I've got a girlfriend.'

'Oh Drew, how lovely, you must bring her next time you come. What's her name, tell me all about her.'

'Her name's Anna and she works in the wine merchants up the road. I've taken her to the pictures twice, but….'

'Yes?'

'She's shy, like me. I don't know if I'm doing or saying the right things 'cause she doesn't say much. I haven't the money to take her out to nice places. The rent's going up again and I'll have even less to spend.'

'Does she like you?'

'I think so, how can you tell?'

'Does she walk apart from you – not look you in the eye, perhaps?'

Lucy felt like an agony aunt.

'No, no. We've held hands, but I haven't, um, kissed her.'

'Oh Drew, you managed to kiss me.' Lucy saw the blood rush to his face and hoped he would soon grow out of that. He was even worse than she was. 'You'll just have to let things take their course. There's plenty you can do without spending a lot of money, walking in the park, for instance. We've plenty of those in South London. Or you could take a bus or train up to town and walk round the West End. If she likes you enough, she won't care where you take her, she'll just want to be with you.'

Drew looked at her wistfully. 'You don't know what it's like to be shy.'

Lucy shook her head forcefully. 'Oh, but I do. My mother used to bully me so much I had no confidence, not even in the things I knew I could do well. I'll tell you something. It was you who gave me some of the self-assurance I had been seeking.'

'Me!' Drew stared at her in disbelief. 'You're just saying that.'

'It's true. I was really down in the dumps when I first came to that room. I'd learned that the father I'd been told was dead could still be alive, and the only boyfriend I'd had dumped me for someone else and told me he felt sorry for me.'

'I can't imagine anyone not loving you.'

'My mother didn't, and she always told me nobody else would and I believed her. What do you think that does to a person? So when I thought I'd found happiness, I discovered that she'd been right all along.'

'Where do I come in all this?'

'It was seeing you so nervous and self-conscious. I knew what you were going through and I saw me in you. I admired you because you plucked up courage and made the first move. You assumed I was full of self-confidence, didn't you?'

'Well, yes.'

'So I thought if that's what you think I am, that's how I'll act, and how you act is how people treat you – on the whole.' Lucy thought about Peter and the odious Mr Crushin. 'Now I try to act as if I'm confident, even if I'm not.' Drew's face was serious as he took in what she said. 'You tell your Anna that you haven't much money, but you like her a lot and would she go for a walk somewhere. Suggest a picnic, she'll probably offer to do the food and if things don't work out, put it down to experience, like I've had to.'

'You are wonderful, Lucy. You're the nicest person I've ever met.'

'Apart from Anna,' Lucy said.

Drew laughed and drained his coffee. 'I'd better be going now. I've to be up early tomorrow. I've had a lovely evening, thank you. It was so good seeing you again.'

They went down the stairs to the hall. 'One more thing, Drew. Always treat a woman with respect. Not every girl is waiting to be taken to bed.'

Drew's astonished look made her smile. 'Sorry, it's that voice of experience speaking.'

She opened the front door. Putting her arms round Drew she gave him a hug and a kiss, just as Peter arrived in the porch.

'Hello, Peter,' she said, moving to one side, 'Go and get yourself a drink while I see Drew out.'

CHAPTER 11

Lucy took in the blazing eyes and tight lines round Peter's mouth as she sat opposite, holding the drink he had poured for her. He hadn't spoken a word.

'You were kissing him,' he said at last.

'Well observed, Sherlock.'

'Why?'

''Cause I felt like it. Why do you kiss girls?'

'I don't anymore.'

'Poor Peter. Aren't they queuing up like they used to?'

'I don't want any girls, I want you.'

'What for?'

'What do you mean what for? What was he doing here anyway?'

'I invited him to dinner.'

'Dinner! He's been here all the evening?'

'Is there some law against it?'

'You never told me.'

'Chance would have been a fine thing. You've hardly spoken to me for over a week. Why should I tell you? I don't need your permission.'

'Because – because…'

'Because you think you own me. The way I was treated by that creep Crushin and your condoning it was despicable. If that's what you think of me, I don't want any more to do with you other than work. Now if you've finished your investigations, you can go.'

The fury on his face showed as he gripped the arms of the chair. His mouth worked as if he were trying to find words, but he was shocked into silence. To justify himself? To blame her? But, she was sure, not to apologise.

'Goodnight. You can see yourself out, can't you?'

Lucy sat for a long time after he'd stormed out. She sipped her drink and her anger slowly died to be replaced by a desolate bleakness. Peter professed to love her, but he'd not discovered what love meant. Women were a game to him. Some you won, some you lost, but there was always another game. What was her destiny? Someone to be sorry for or someone to be controlled and manipulated? But never a woman to be loved for herself.

*

Stephen Holloway was in a quandary. He should have done something about it at the end of the summer term, but after all the trouble Ted had gone through, he couldn't bring himself to deal with the matter as he should have done. He had hoped the summer break might have seen Ted rested and recovering from his loss. Surely a year was long enough. After all, it wasn't as if she were his wife. But now complaints were coming in from parents about lack of homework set, or not marked properly, if at all. Concerned staff reported passing his classroom where the noise was such that the children seemed out of control.

Stephen had come across Ted periodically and had already noticed how much weight he'd lost, but as he sat before him now, he could see at close quarters the alarming deterioration in the man. Ted's face was florid, but his cheeks were hollow, his eyes half-closed as if he were having difficulty concentrating.

'Before you say anything, Stephen, I'm intending to give in my notice. I should have done it in May, I know.'

'I don't think you need go to that extreme, you're a good teacher.'

'Was - my heart's no longer in it and, as you were no doubt intending to tell me, it's affecting my work.'

'Yes, that was what I was going to say.'

Stephen's secretary came in with a tray and put it on the desk His hand shook as he took a cup from her and the Head noticed the wool unravelling at the cuff of his green sweater.

'What notice can I give? I've missed the deadline to leave at the end of October.'

Relieved he hadn't had to make an unpleasant decision, Stephen said, 'We could no doubt cite extenuating circumstances, ill-health for instance.'

Ted took a sip from the cup, replaced it on the saucer and rattled it back to the tray. 'If you think that would be best,' he said, standing up. 'Have I to wait till half term – or shall I go now.'

The Head couldn't help comparing this situation with that at the time of the Cromer affair. 'The end of the day would be best.'

At the door Ted turned. 'By the way, Lorraine Cromer passed

her 'A' level at evening classes – with a B.'

*

'Can you spare me a minute?' Lucy said, poking her head round Peter's office door.

'Sit down, Miss Daniels.'

'No need to overdo the cold shoulder. Nobody calls me that.'

'So I've noticed. Well, what d'you want?'

'I've had an idea. How about a crèche?'

'A crèche!' Peter stared at Lucy as if she were about to give birth to its first occupant.

'What's so startling about that? The government's all in favour.'

'We're here to do business, not run a benevolent institution.'

'But you don't realise what difficulties some of these women work under. They nearly all have children and they have to work to earn enough money just to exist. If there's no one at home, they need to pay a childminder, and they don't come cheap. And, from what I've been told, some of them leave a lot to be desired.'

'And where is this crèche going to be – on the roof?'

'I can see there's not enough room here,' Lucy said, exasperated by his deliberate attempt not to understand. 'We have to expand the workforce now we're getting more business, and with this facility it'll be easier to attract new workers. We could get together with other offices and factories on the site.'

'We've never had a problem getting women to work here. They're glad to get a job at all. Why do they have kids if they can't afford them?'

'That's how you exploit them and keep their wages at the minimum.'

'We're competitive.' Peter went back to the sheaf of papers in front of him and cast his eye up and down a sheet of paper attempting to look engrossed.

'Can I put it to David and your mother? Get their opinions?'

'No,' he said, without raising his head. 'It's out of the question. I've too much on my plate to even think about it.' Emily came into the room. 'Go away,' he shouted, before she had a chance to speak.

'Don't take it out on her,' Lucy said, as Emily retreated.

'Don't tell me what I can and can't do in my own office!'

'Sorry, I thought I was part of the business.'

'No. I employed you to do what I want you to do, not think

104

up crazy, unnecessary and unworkable schemes.'

Deflated and hurt by his attitude, Lucy went back to her office. Picking up two files she went to Accounts. 'Look over these figures for me, will you, Gordon? I've got to visit this firm so I need to have my facts correct. They're very rough estimates, so I'm sure you'll have plenty of comments.'

He gave her a brief smile. 'OK, leave them there.'

Lynne glared. She was the only enemy Lucy had made and she wished she hadn't been quite so speedy doing Lynne's work when she was ill. Now Peter was enemy number two. When she left Gordon's office she strolled over to the girls. She missed them and their news.

Joy beckoned her over, a broad grin showing up her white teeth in her jolly face.

'Here, wanna hear the latest joke my boy told me? What do you call a three-legged donkey?' Lucy shook her head. 'Wonkey.'

A shriek of laughter rose above the noise of the machinery. As it died away, a voice called loudly across the factory floor.

'I didn't employ you to stop the girls working. Even if you have no work of your own, in future confine yourself to the offices.'

The blood rushed to Lucy's face as she stood mortified. The girls put their heads down, too embarrassed to look at her. She stood for some moments unable to move till she heard someone mutter, 'Who rattled his cage? Bet you're glad you're not married to him.'

Anger overwhelmed her like flames consuming a bonfire. She strode over to Peter's office and flung open the door. Emily was taking notes.

'Give me a few minutes, please Emily.'

Lucy, grim faced, leaned against the open door waiting for her to leave. When it had shut behind her, Lucy advanced into the room.

'How dare you? How dare you shout at me like that in front of everybody,' she exploded. 'Just because you can't coerce or wheedle me into doing what you want, you're wreaking vengeance by humiliating me. You are detestable.'

Lucy had never felt such anger. She held on to the edge of his desk, her legs trembling. This is how her mother had made her feel, and resentment at Peter recalling past humiliations was added to her fury. Her throat tightened and her eyes were stinging, but she was not going to give him the satisfaction of witnessing a weakness he would exploit. She leaned forward till Peter's face was so close she could see the flecks in his irises.

'I hate you,' she spat out with such venom he recoiled. 'How I thought I could love you, I do not know.'

Lucy returned to her office aware of eyes observing her, contemplating, no doubt, an interesting few days ahead. How long she sat at her desk she had no idea - twenty minutes, half an hour – but she was unable to rouse herself. Gordon came in and Lucy wearily pushed herself forward in her chair.

'These may be rough estimates, but they appear pretty accurate to me. I've made one or two amendments and – are you all right?'

'I've had a little upset.'

'Something you ought to see a doctor about?' he asked, concerned.

Lucy shook her head. No need to disillusion him about her health, he would learn the reason soon enough.

'Well, look after yourself. I'm finding you quite indispensable.'

She smiled weakly. It was nice to be highly esteemed by someone, but lurking at the back of her mind was the thought she could no longer work with Peter. He was too close to ignore emotionally and from a business point of view. Denise's words came back to haunt her. *What are the pitfalls he's choosing not to tell you?* Now she knew. If things did not go as he wanted, he could make her life unbearable.

Next day even the late shift was aware of the row. Lucy mouthed her usual Good Morning as she waved, and went to her office, wondering as she did so what they were thinking. Sympathy? Pity? Or perhaps they were looking forward to another confrontation to brighten up their monotonous existence. Lucy didn't blame them. She took files from the drawer and spread them in front of her. She had to talk to Peter some time today; she couldn't put it off. Information was needed on the company she had to visit. Concentrating on the work in front of her, she didn't hear Lynne come in.

'Your coffee,' Lynne said, placing the cup as far from Lucy's reach as she could get it. Lynne had resented having to make her a drink from her very first day, and now having to bring it to her office was an added insult.

'Hello, Lynne, how are things with you?'

'All right.'

She wondered if working with Gordon Ross had made Lynne less talkative. It seemed the more Gordon communicated, the less Lynne had to say, if that were possible. She contemplated asking after her boyfriend, but having to listen to her monosyllabic answers was something Lucy wasn't up to at the moment. As she reached for her cup she noticed a smirk on Lynne's face.

'Was there something else you wanted?'

'No.' She hesitated, and Lucy tipped her head to one side expectantly, pretty certain what was coming next.

'I heard Mr Evans was in a bad mood yesterday.'

'Yes, I heard the same. Better not cross his path then, eh, Lynne?' Lucy smiled sweetly and Lynne departed with her usual disgruntled expression, mixed with disappointment that Lucy hadn't been embarrassed.

At two o'clock, Lucy made a point of seeing Joy to apologise if she had caused them any trouble.

'I shan't come over so often, but don't think I'm deserting you. I can always see you in the Ladies.'

With some trepidation, she went to see Peter.

'I need to discuss the background to Blackmore's before I visit. Can you fill me in?'

'Can't you find out for yourself?'

'Yes, but don't you think it would be easier for you to give me the low down. It was you who spoke to them so you have it to hand. I'd have to ring up and they'd think it pretty funny you hadn't passed it on.' Ball in your court Peter Evans.

He went over to the filing cabinet and took out a thin, buff file. While he exaggeratedly sorted through it, extracting and replacing papers, prolonging the time he'd have to deal with her, she studied his face. Tight-lipped, brows drawn, eyes flitting from side to side. He raised his head and caught her scrutiny, but couldn't hold her gaze. He cleared his throat.

'Tony Blackmore was a friend of my father's. His nephew took over when he retired. We haven't done any business with them for some years but I thought, as they'd diversified into time control mechanisms, they might be able to give us some contacts, even if they haven't anything for us themselves.'

'I hardly think they're going to give us any help if we're going to be competitors.'

'Just give it a try, will you?' he said tersely.

'If he was a friend of your father's, wouldn't it be better if you went to this one and I contacted someone else.'

'Do you have to question everything I do?'

'I just thought if you knew the nephew, it seems obvious....'

'I don't know him. It was my father who knew his uncle.'

'All right, all right, I'll do what you say. May I have the file to study?" Peter appeared reluctant to hand it over. Eventually he stuffed the loose papers inside and slid it across his desk. 'Here. Put those sheets back while you're at it.'

'Peter?'

'Yes.'

'Why are you treating me like this? I can't go on working in this atmosphere.'

'You can always leave.'

*

David looked up from his desk. 'What's up, Lucy?'

'I'm giving in my notice.'

'Is it Peter? I heard about your confrontation.'

'You and everybody else.'

'If what I heard was right, it was unforgivable, and you should have told him so.'

'I did.'

'Good for you, but you don't want to go leaving. You're much too good and Peter knows it. He'll simmer down, he always does.'

'It goes deeper than that; it isn't just work. You see, he wants me – he wants to have an affair and I won't. This is the only way he can get back at me and I can't work like that.'

This girl is certainly made of stern stuff. Peter had known her well over a year, yet all those weekends at his house and the days they'd been away together, he had failed to seduce her. Something strange was going on in that head of his. The lad was falling in love and didn't know how to deal with it. No wonder he was in such a bad way.

David came round the desk and took her hand. 'I'll have a word with him....'

'No, no! You're not to tell him what I said about – it was confidential.'

'I'll keep it strictly business.' They moved towards the door. 'He wouldn't accept your resignation anyway.'

'He suggested it.'

'What!' David's handsome face contorted and strands of his

silvery hair fell forward as he shook his head in angry disbelief.

Lucy was frightened by his expression. 'Please don't say anything to him. It'll make things worse.' She put out her arm to try to stop him as he neared the door.

'Lucy always manages to find comfort in some man's arms, I find,' Peter said as he stood in the office doorway.

David pushed Lucy away and grabbed the lapels of Peter's suit. With a crash he was rammed against a filing cabinet.

'If I ever hear you speak to, or about Lucy in such a way again, you'll have me to answer to, d'you hear?' He thrust him harder against the cabinet, David's face almost touching Peter's. 'It's obvious you've never met any decent women in your life because you sure as hell don't know how to treat them.'

He released him and Peter tried to compose himself, straightening his jacket and running his fingers through his hair.

'Now, get back to your office and concentrate on making the firm a success, like the rest of the workforce is trying to do.'

Peter adjusted his tie and walked unsteadily to the door as David returned to his desk. 'And leave Lucy alone. She's worth two of you,' he shouted after him.

It was then that David realised Lucy was no longer in the room.

*

'Where's Peter?' Lucy asked Emily next morning.

'He's not in yet. He went home early yesterday because he didn't feel well.'

I bet he did, she thought. 'OK, let me know when he arrives.'

Lucy had not stayed to hear all David had to say. She thought he was going to punch Peter and she didn't want to be around if he did. She had not thought David capable of such fury.

By twelve, Peter had still not appeared and David asked Emily to ring him, but she said there was no reply.

'I'll call in on my way home, David,' Lucy said. 'I expect he's having a sulk.'

'And well he might. I won't have him treating you like the tramps he's used to.'

There was no answer to the bell when she reached his house. She peered in the windows in the front and the back and tried the back door. Then she stood back to survey the upstairs windows.

Returning to the front she tried the bell again. Lucy was about to return to her car when she remembered she had a key Peter had given her, but had never used. She rummaged in her bag.

'Peter, you there?' she shouted from the hall. All was quiet. He must have gone out shopping or for a walk. In the kitchen she hunted for paper and a pencil.

> Peter
>
> *We were worried about you as you hadn't rung. I expect you'll be in tomorrow. Hope you're better.*
>
> Lucy

She propped it against the toaster.

As she was about to step into her car, she took one last look at the house. Was that a curtain moving? She frowned. But all the windows were closed so it couldn't be the breeze. Funny, there had been no sound when she'd called. Lucy went back into the house and looked in all the rooms – then upstairs.

CHAPTER 12

He was under the bedroom window slumped to one side where he had fallen from a sitting position. Lucy rushed over and knelt down. 'Peter, Peter, what's the matter?'

His eyes were closed and his dry lips opened as if to speak, but no sound came. His forehead glistened with sweat.

'Your doctor? Who's your doctor?' Lucy hauled him back into a sitting position and pulled the sheet off the bed and put it round his bare shoulders; the duvet she piled round him so he could hardly be seen. She flew downstairs to search for an address book, which she found in the bureau.

After ringing a doctor she contacted Peter's mother.

'Mrs Evans, Peter's ill. I found him on the floor of his bedroom. I've sent for a doctor, the one I found in a book, but he hasn't arrived yet.'

'What's wrong?'

'He's feverish and in a sort of coma. He doesn't recognise me and he looks awful.'

'Shall I come up?'

'Don't do anything yet, Mrs Evans. I'll ring you – ah, there's the bell, that'll be the doctor. I'll get back to you. Bye.'

Dr Bellerby, case in hand, followed Lucy up the stairs. 'I couldn't get him back into bed, doctor. I don't think he'd been on the floor a long time because the sheets were still warm.'

The doctor knelt down and pulled the duvet from Peter's face. 'Peter, can you hear me?' There was no response. He felt for his pulse then took out a slim torch and lifting each eyelid shone it into his eyes. 'Let's get him back into bed.'

'What do you think is wrong?' she asked, anxiously, as they struggled to lift him up. Lucy explained about his leaving work with a headache, and why she was there.

'It was a good job you were, Miss....'

'Daniels.'

'He is running a very high temperature, but I'm not sure

111

what's wrong yet. Could be a bad bout of flu, could be a viral infection or even meningitis.'

'Meningitis!' Lucy exclaimed. 'Isn't that serious?'

'Could be, but there's no need to panic just yet.' He smiled reassuringly.

Lucy was already panicking. 'What shall I do?'

'Has he been vomiting?'

'I don't know, I found him where you found him and rang you almost immediately.'

The doctor felt round Peter's neck and he gave a faint groan. 'Wring out a cloth in cold water and cool him down,' he instructed.

Lucy went into the bathroom to return a few moments later to confirm that Peter had been sick. Dr Bellerby was pressing a glass against Peter's arm and peering at his skin.

'Right, young lady, keep the curtains closed and have as dim a light as possible. Keep sponging his face and make him drink as he'll be dehydrated. I'll come in tomorrow but if you're worried, ring me at home. It's not meningitis, but it looks nasty whatever it is.'

Lucy sat by the bed all night wiping Peter's face and trying to make him drink. About three he began muttering, slowly moving his head and groaning. His face appeared blotchy, but the only light was from the landing, so she wasn't sure. She dozed fitfully, afraid to go to sleep in case there should be some drastic change.

At nine next morning Peter's mother arrived.

'You look dreadful,' she said to Lucy. 'Have you had any sleep?'

'Cat naps. The doctor should be here soon, I'll just wait to see what he says, then I must get to work.'

'You found Graham Bellerby's number then?'

'It was the only number there for a doctor, so I chanced it. Go on up.' As Lucy turned towards the stairs, the doctor arrived.

'Hello, Graham,' Eleanor said, as she leaned over the banister. 'It's a long time since I've seen you.'

'Eleanor, you're looking well. Let's see how that son of yours has progressed since yesterday.'

He followed her to the bedroom and Lucy joined them.

'How's he been?' he asked Lucy.

'He's had a restless night, but hasn't been sick again. I've had difficulty making him drink,' she told him.

'His temperature's down a mite,' the doctor said, peering at the thermometer, 'but he's still feverish. It seems a particularly virulent bug. I had a similar case last week, and the patient is still very weak. Continue as you've been doing – lots to drink and keep him cool. I'll come in tomorrow, but I'm sure he'll have surfaced by then.' He smiled at them both and touched Eleanor's arm. 'He'll be OK.'

Back at the factory after reporting to David, she went to see Emily who said Peter had an appointment with a client next day. It wasn't for new business, more a courtesy call, taking him out to lunch and assuring him our firm was the greatest thing since the landing on the moon. Examining her face in the mirror, Lucy thought he'd think she'd just landed, and hoped she would get more sleep tonight.

'How is he?' she asked Mrs Evans that evening as she hung her coat on the hallstand.

'He seems to be out of his coma, but drifts in and out of sleep. He knows who I am. Doctor's been and gone.'

Peter lay as still as a corpse. His arms, palms down, stuck out rigidly on top of the covers and his face was drawn and dark with the stubble of two days' growth. She approached the bed and took his hand. He didn't move, but murmured, 'She wouldn't come. Lucy wouldn't come.'

'I'm here now.'

He turned his head and opened his eyes. 'Why didn't you come? I called and called.'

'I did come. You moved the curtain and I saw it.' Lucy pushed his hair back and wiped his forehead. She poured some water from the jug. 'Here, drink this.'

'I heard you – downstairs – I got out of bed and called – but you wouldn't come.'

'I did come, Peter.' He gave a weak smile and closed his eyes. 'The doctor says you'll soon feel better.'

After a meal that Mrs Evans had prepared for her, Lucy said she would get some sleep. 'When you feel you want to go to bed, call me, Mrs Evans.'

It was nearly midnight when she went to Peter's bedroom. He patted a place beside him. 'Lay down beside me, Lucy. Mother told me you hardly had any sleep last night. If I feel bad, I'll wake you.'

He moved over and gratefully she climbed up beside him.

'I was so worried about you when I found you on the floor.'

'Were you? I thought you hated me.'

'I did when I said it. Now you must go to sleep.'

Lucy woke about four. The house was very quiet, only the low murmur of London traffic could be heard. She turned to see if Peter were sleeping. 'Are you all right?' she asked softly when she could see he was awake.

'Yes.' He felt for her hand. 'I'm sorry.'

'For being ill?'

'No, for shouting at you like I did.'

'Let's wait until you feel well before you say any more. You need your rest, and I've got to work, and do yours as well.'

'What of mine have you to do?'

'See a Mr Greenley and tell him we still love him Emily said.'

'Oh, yes, I remember.' He paused. 'He's a flirt.'

Lucy's heart sunk. 'Not another one?'

'Much nicer than Crushin. More charm.'

Lucy raised herself on one elbow and peered at him suspiciously. 'How d'you know he's a flirt?'

'I've seen him in action.'

'No female is safe with you two. Is he married with four children as well?'

Peter gave a feeble laugh and Lucy noticed small beads of perspiration on his upper lip.

'You're tiring yourself. You're very ill, you know.'

'Give me a kiss so I'll have sweet dreams.'

'I've been giving you lots of kisses.'

'Have you?' He looked pleased. 'But this one I want to know about.'

Lucy put her arm across his body and gently kissed him. He closed his eyes and was asleep in seconds.

When she reached Peter's next evening he was sitting up in bed. His mother had shaved him making him more presentable.

'What have you been doing?' Lucy asked.

'A lot of sleeping, listening to the radio, talking to my mother. Bellerby's been and won't be coming again for a few days. Keep taking the pills and make sure I hang on to Miss Daniels he said.'

'He didn't say that,' she said sceptically.

'He did.' He leaned forward and took her hand. 'Pull your chair closer.'

'Peter, I don't want you to say anything, not until you've completely recovered.'

'But I've something I want to say to you.'

114

'When you're better.' She saw the familiar knitted brows. 'Humour me?' Lucy felt his hand tremble in hers as Peter fell back on his pillow. He was much weaker than he thought and she didn't want him to make any decisions that might not have the result he expected.

'I'm going downstairs. Your mother's getting me something to eat.'

'Will you be sleeping beside me tonight?'

'I don't think that's necessary.' She grinned and he pulled a face.

Mrs Evans was sitting in the drawing room, a large cardboard box at her feet. Photographs lay scattered on a low table that she had pulled up in front of her. A neater pile was on a small marquetry table by the arm of her chair.

'You sit down there, Lucy.'

She left the room returning with a plate of cold ham and beef and a baked potato.

'I found this box in the dining room.' Peter's mother said. 'He must have got it down after all, I thought he'd forgotten. It's surprising how many photographs one collects over the years. I've never got around to putting them in albums.'

'Got any of Peter when he was little?'

'There are these when he was about ten.'

She handed Lucy a wallet and she looked at the curly headed boy with a cheeky grin. 'That was taken about the time I had a miscarriage.'

'How awful.'

'I had three altogether. I never wanted only one child.'

There were pictures of relatives, of the three of them on holiday, Peter playing cricket and Mrs Evans holding a crab. Lucy studied the photo to see if there were any resemblance between Peter and his father, but he didn't appear to look much like either of his parents – perhaps a little like his mother.

'Does Peter take after his father?' Lucy always studied people with their fathers, it was an obsession of hers grown, no doubt, from the absence of her own.

'In looks?'

'No, I was thinking more in temperament.'

'They both had great charm, but with Peter you never know what he might do next. Jack wasn't *quite* so headstrong.' She stopped speaking and gazed unseeing over Lucy's head. 'Though he did have a spell of depression....'

Lucy waited for her to continue, but her thoughts seemed to drift and she continued removing photos from the box. Lucy supposed it was the time that David had told her about when the factory was in financial trouble.

It was after nine. Lucy had finished her meal and said she would get them both a drink. When she came back, Mrs Evans had almost emptied the box. 'That'll do. I'll show these to my ladies. Peter can put the box back in the loft when he's better. How is he?'

'He was nearly asleep when I took his drink up. He still looks weak, don't you think?'

'I can see our next problem will be keeping him in bed and resting, and then stopping him from doing too much once he's up.'

'I won't be coming tomorrow,' Lucy informed her. 'I must go home to do a few neglected chores. Don't mention it to Peter until you have to. He'll be put out.'

'You seem to know how to handle him.'

'Maybe,' she said, fingering her bracelet.

Handling him was not the main problem.

*

Peter said, 'My mother has gone home, I can make a cup of tea all by myself and the doctor says I can go back to work next week. Now may I speak to you?'

Peter had been off work for three weeks and, contrary to what his mother had thought, he'd followed to the letter everything the doctor had advised.

'You know what I want to say, don't you?' He reached for her hand and held it in both his. 'Will you marry me?'

Gently he moved his thumb across the back of her hand. Moments passed but Peter did not raise his eyes.

'No,' she said at last. 'I don't think it would work.'

Peter's face, pale and drawn, was bewildered. 'Is it because I'm moody and bad-tempered?'

'No, I think I could cope. I lived with my mother, remember, and managed to survive for twenty years.'

'You don't love me then.'

'I do. Seeing you so ill made me realise.'

'So what is it? Tell me,' he pleaded. He peered deeply into her eyes as if he might see the reason there.

'I can't, I just can't. I'm sorry.' Anxious to escape the look in his eyes she said, 'I'll get us something to eat.'

'No, I'll do it. You've done enough for me these past weeks.'

Lucy saw the desolation in his drooping shoulders as he left the room. She wished he'd put off asking her till he was stronger. Lucy had lain awake at night in this very house, knowing Peter was going to propose. She pictured the comfortable life and the children she would have. She thought of Peter's love for her, which she no longer doubted because she'd seen it in his eyes – that tenderness and affection that Ted had whenever he looked at Catherine. Was she stupid to give that up because she questioned his fidelity once the novelty of marriage had worn off?

'Here we are,' he said, as he put her plate of spaghetti and two glasses on the table in front of her.

Lucy moved a side table beside hers and he returned with his plate and bottle of red wine.

'Is it to your liking?'

'It's very good. I didn't know you could cook so well.'

'There's a lot you don't know about me, mostly the nice things.'

Lucy put down her fork. 'I'm sorry, Peter, I didn't want to hurt you.' She put her hand on his arm; he went on eating. 'Look at me.'

'I can't Lucy. I'll do something I haven't done since I was a child and I'll feel a fool and embarrass you.'

Peter picked up the bottle and the swirling rioja wine sounded extraordinarily loud as he poured. Lucy longed to put her arms round him to comfort and be comforted. How could she explain her feelings without hurting him further?

Back in the drawing room after clearing up, Peter suggested they go through the box of photographs before he put them away again.

'I saw some while your mother was sorting through and she told me about her miscarriages.'

'I think it was a bad time for her, though I wasn't old enough to understand at the time. My father took it badly because the factory wasn't doing well and it depressed him. I didn't know about this till years later when David told me.'

Peter picked up the photos explaining each one, telling her of his relations and which side of the family they were. He named his prep school pals and those who went on with him to Dulwich.

'Are you still in touch with any of them?'

'Not really. I lost contact because I was away from home so

much. One or two still send Christmas cards. They're all married now.' His wistful tone pressed home her rejection.

'You're tired. You mustn't overdo it just because you're feeling a lot better, especially if you're starting work on Monday.'

'I do feel I've had enough.'

'You go up and I'll bring you a drink. Remember what Dr Bellerby said.' She laughed, trying to lighten the gloom that had descended on them. Peter didn't smile and left the room without commenting.

Peter was sitting up in bed, but was almost asleep when she brought him his drink. She sat beside him and put her arm round his shoulders but felt him stiffen as she handed him the mug.

'Don't do that, I can't bear it.'

Quickly she removed her arm. She wondered if a kiss on the forehead would be as unwelcome. As she gazed down at him, hurt by, but understanding his rebuff, she almost gave in. She wanted to smother his face with kisses and lie beside him warm in his arms.

'Night, then, Peter.' She took the mug from him. 'See you in the morning. I'll go back to my flat after breakfast.'

'Very well.' He slid down the bed, pulling the bedclothes over his ears till he was lost from sight.

'I love you,' she whispered as she left.

*

Had she ever been happy Lucy asked herself as she pushed the dirty clothes into the machine? There were the occasions when her exam results had arrived, but these were diluted by rows over staying for 'A' levels and going to university. And there was Ian's invitation to move in with him. But this decision, she later realised, was more a desire for escape than to be with someone she thought loved her. Was it any wonder he'd found someone else? Now she loved a man who loved her and it was she who was refusing his proposal.

Lucy set about the mounds of junk mail and letters that had accumulated. Mechanically she searched for her chequebook and dealt with the bills, putting a first class stamp on the final demand. There were three other letters. One, mildly reproving was from her grandmother. The other two, in much the same vein, were from Ted in rather shaky handwriting, and from Denise. Their concern and her guilt at not keeping in touch brought tears to her eyes. Today she should be joyful, ecstatic. Instead Lucy could only picture the hurt in Peter's eyes and his cold expression as they sat over a near-silent breakfast.

The washing machine whirred its final spin. She took out the clothes and put in the next load. Lucy wandered into her former bedroom, her little cocoon where she sought refuge when her mother was being particularly oppressive. Running her hand along the top of the chest of drawers she peered at the dust on her fingertips. What would her mother have said about that?

The bay-fronted living room reflected her mother's taste. As soon as she could she would fling herself into changing it. There would be plenty of time now. No more visits to Dulwich; no more business trips. What would they say to each other tomorrow? How could she alleviate his pain without giving in? Was she foolish even to think about what might go wrong in a marriage? Marriage was a gamble however it was viewed, but Lucy could not risk being hurt yet again. Better to suffer now than when she had a home, children and a husband she loved.

*

The house seemed bigger, more silent with Lucy gone. Silly, Peter thought, he had lived here alone for three years, why should it now seem like a large empty shell rather than his comfortable home?

His frustration recalled a time when he asked his father to take him fishing after seeing a television programme. All the equipment was hired and one hot, sunny day they headed off. Peter couldn't remember where, only the excitement of doing something he wanted to do.

Neither of them knew anything about fishing, but his father eventually managed get a line in the water without it getting caught on nearby branches. Peter was bored after two hours when the novelty had worn off and the fish hadn't shared his enthusiasm. He told his father he wanted to go home. Then the line jerked and he yelled as he reeled in.

'Dad, Dad, look. It's a whopper.'

The fish neared the bank swishing its tail, but as his father held the net to catch it, the fish slipped the hook and swam away. Peter cried with frustration, jumping up and down in a rage. This vivid memory summed up his feelings as he had coolly kissed Lucy on the cheek and shut the door on her – the equivalent of jumping up and down in a rage. It must be his bad temper that had made her turn him down, in spite of her denials. He was sulky and childish, always expecting and getting his own way. Had she not told him so?

Lucy hadn't had much good fortune in her life. No father, unloved and ill treated by her mother; a boyfriend who preferred someone else. What he wouldn't give to have been in Ian's shoes. Surely Lucy could see all he could offer. Tomorrow and every day they would have to face each other and he couldn't imagine how he would cope. He felt an overwhelming attraction for her. He loved her. He had tried to deny it; tried to think of her as he had his other passing fancies, but she wouldn't fit into the mould. She was Lucy – his Lucy.

*

At the factory on Monday everybody had shaken his hand and told him how pleased they were to see him back. Lucy hoped she had managed to carry out her position as assistant to the boss without showing her true feelings. They all knew she had found him, that she had stayed the night and had called from time to time to visit and report back. Only David knew that she'd been at his house practically every evening. Lucy forced a smile when Peter took her hand and she said how delighted she was to see him back. Emily had a chaste kiss and told him she had missed him terribly. Peter said he didn't know she cared, and made her blush.

Later that morning Peter brought his coffee into Lucy's office. 'I've come to apologise – yet again.'

'Apologise? What for?'

'The childish way I behaved.'

Lucy put out her hand. 'It's me who should be apologising. I just can't make the commitment you want.'

'But why? I don't understand if you say you love me.' There was that childlike look of bewilderment. For all his sophistication and self-assurance, Lucy noticed how unsettled he had become.

'It's not that I couldn't cope with you. I might even succeed in calming you down, though I wouldn't bet on it.' She pressed the hand under hers. 'But – but….' She broke off, unwilling to explain.

'Let's go to lunch then we can talk some more.'

'I've brought sandwiches. I'm very behind with my own work.'

'Of course, I didn't think.' Peter sat motionless, gazing into his cup. 'Aren't you going to see me anymore?'

'I don't think that's a good idea. You could hardly bear me to touch you on Saturday night, and I'm not sure I could stand it either.'

Lucy felt like crying, and wished he'd go back to his own office before she did.

That week at the factory was one of the worst Peter had experienced. Lucy, he knew, was avoiding him whenever she could, always out at lunch time and leaving without saying goodbye as she usually did. He rang on several evenings, but she was either out or engaged. He found it difficult to get into any routine and by mid afternoon he was exhausted. On Friday, Emily urged him to go home early and, reluctant though he was to give in, he had done just that.

Peter slept till ten on Saturday morning and in an effort to overcome his depression, he went up to town.

CHAPTER 13

It had started to drizzle adding to his despondency, and Peter pulled up the collar of his coat as he left the station. He strolled into the Strand, through the queuing taxis, heading he knew not where. A show perhaps, not that that would be much fun on his own. Still, he might as well do something now he was here. He turned back towards the station to buy a newspaper. He felt in his pocket for change when a woman's voice called, 'Peter? Peter Evans?'

His head jerked up recognising the low, husky voice, but for a second unable to place it. 'Stephanie! Good heavens, Stephanie.' Peter's face lit up. 'Fancy seeing you. How are you? What are you doing now?'

After a few minutes questioning each other, Stephanie said, 'Look, we can't talk here. You off anywhere in particular? Shall we find somewhere we can chat?'

When they discovered neither had any commitment for the evening they went for a meal. Peter noticed she still caught the eye of every man.

'You know, you don't look a day older,' Peter said when they had ordered. He studied her clear skin, perfect features, blonde loosely waved shoulder-length hair and her large, brown eyes.

'Flatterer. I'm twenty-eight.'

'Still footloose and fancy free?' Peter asked.

She hunched her shoulders. 'More or less. I'm in a flat in Chelsea paid for by my lover. He's married – wife doesn't understand him – usual thing. He knows the score.' Her voice was full of contempt. 'What about you? Still on the rigs?'

'No, I gave that up some years ago. My father died and my mother wanted me to take over the company.'

'Why haven't you got in touch?' She didn't wait for an answer. 'You look a lot thinner.'

'I haven't been well.' He told her about his illness, mentioning Lucy in passing.

'So, you've not settled down. I wouldn't have minded marrying you myself, except I'm not the marrying kind. We had some good times, didn't we?'

Over the meal they chatted about their families and what they'd done since they'd last met. When they reached coffee, Stephanie put out her hand and lightly touched his.

'You're not happy, are you Peter? You never could hide your emotions.'

Feeling he had to talk to someone, he unburdened himself. He told her how he'd met this timid girl seeking her father, how he'd persuaded her to join his firm and then fallen in love with her.

'Why aren't you living together then?'

'I've asked her to marry me, but she won't.'

Stephanie pouted. 'You never asked me.'

'Lucy won't say,' he went on. 'I think it's because she thinks I'd be difficult to live with 'cause I do have a quick temper, though she says that's not why. I shouted at her in front of the whole shop floor a few weeks back.'

'And what did she do?'

'She bawled me out – in private. She's much too nice to humiliate me in public. And,' he went on, 'she nursed me for several nights while I was ill and then went to work next day.'

'And she says she doesn't love you?' Stephanie exclaimed.

'No, no, she says she does,' he stared gloomily into his cup. 'But obviously not enough to marry me.'

'I see,' she said slowly, sipping the last of her coffee.

'Can you think why?' he asked hopefully.

Stephanie picked up a mint and Peter watched as her long, red tipped fingers slowly unwrapped it. She took a bite, showing her perfect teeth. As she smoothed the green silver paper, she said, 'Yes.'

'You can! Well tell me.'

'Does she know about your previous girlfriends.'

'Yes.'

'Have you been to bed with her?'

'No, not for want of trying,' he said, giving her a saucy grin.

Stephanie's beautiful eyes opened wide, and she let out a tinkling laugh. He used to love her laugh; she was always fun to be with and a great lover. Peter shook himself; he didn't want to think about the past - only about Lucy.

'So, what's your opinion? If I know what's bugging her, I

might be able to do something about it.'

'You might, but I don't think you can.'

'Why? What's wrong with me?'

'This Lucy sounds like a one man girl to me and....'

'You mean – you mean she doesn't think I'll be faithful?' His tone was incredulous as if no one could possibly think such a thing.

'Peter, let's face it, you and I are two of a kind. Not for us a home and kids. We want variety, excitement. You'll get restless, crave the life you once had and this Lucy can sense this.' She examined his face. 'You don't think so?'

Peter stared at the wall behind Stephanie, painted to represent a balcony with distant views of Tuscan hills. She rose from her chair and a waiter appeared from nowhere to hold her coat, hovering long after it was buttoned. She gave him the benefit of a smile. Peter felt a stirring, a longing for times past. His celibate life had been going on far too long. Lucy couldn't really love him. If she had, she would have given way long ago.

'Peter. You haven't been listening. I said, do you want to come back to my place?'

'What about your man?'

'He's abroad.'

When they reached her block of flats near Sloane Square, he paid off the taxi. They went in the lift to the top floor and along the thick carpeted corridor to flat nine. Whoever Stephanie's lover was, he wasn't short of money.

The flat was expensively but sparsely furnished. A small modern black dining table stood in the window with four matching chairs. There were two leather armchairs, also black, on either side of a glass-topped coffee table. A mock marble mantelpiece surrounded an elaborate electric fire. A long, low sideboard completed the furnishings. All was extraordinarily neat like an exhibition show flat. Peter smiled, surmising that that was just what it was.

'Get yourself a drink and one for me.' She nodded towards the sideboard and disappeared into what Peter assumed was a bedroom.

'This is a comfy pad,' he called to her. 'You'd better hold on to this one.'

'As long as I can, then his wife will find out and give him some ultimatum and it'll be over – then I'll move on.'

This was said with such lack of guile that he had to smile.

Stephanie came back into the room.

'Here's your drink.' He pointed to the glass on the table.

'You remembered.'

'I don't think I've forgotten anything about you.'

She patted his knee as she passed him. 'Nor I you.'

'So what do you think I ought to do about Lucy?'

'Nothing,' she said shortly. 'She's made her position clear, she loves you but she doesn't want to marry you – so that's that.'

'But…'

'Come on Peter, you've got to forget her. I'll help you.' She gave him a seductive smile. 'When we've finished our drinks, let's renew old times.'

The temptation was irresistible; his need compelling. It wouldn't mean anything, would it? It would be as it used to be. But wouldn't that prove Stephanie right – and Lucy.

'No, now you've told me what's wrong, I'm going to try again.'

'It was only a theory,' she began, pushing out her lips.

'I can't let her go, I love her too much.'

'Well you have changed,' she drawled. 'I never thought I'd hear you talk about love. Your love is sex, I know it and your Lucy knows it.'

'No it isn't,' he snapped. 'I want her for my wife and I want children, lots of them and I want her to be their mother.'

'If you say so. She must be some woman this Lucy of yours.'

Peter finished the last of his drink, stood up and put his glass on the table. 'I'll be going.' He bent and kissed her forehead. 'It really was good seeing you again.'

Stephanie did not see him out.

*

'I haven't seen you for months, Lucy dear,' her grandmother said reproachfully. 'What have you been doing? Where've you been?'

'Peter's been ill and I've been so busy, but I've no excuse really, Nana. I'll see more of you now, I promise.'

'How do you like living in your mother's flat?'

'I lived there for nineteen years,' she said tersely. 'It was my flat, too.'

'Yes, of course, dear. I didn't mean anything.' She tailed off.

'Sorry, Nana. I'm beginning to sound like my mother, aren't I? The flat's fine, better than that room in Lewisham. I'm going to buy some new furniture – a three-piece suite I think, new cushions, a carpet perhaps. I've started painting the kitchen.'

Lucy prattled on trying to find things to say that might stop her grandmother asking questions she didn't want to think about, let alone answer.

'How's Peter? Has he asked you to marry him yet?' Her grandmother looked at her hopefully. Life was very simple to Nana and nothing would please her more than to see Lucy married. But what could she say? Yes, but I refused – no, he's just a friend? Whether she took Lucy's silence to mean things were not going well, she didn't know, but her grandmother didn't pursue it.

'Found out anything about your father?'

'No. A detective agency Peter contacted said there wasn't enough to go on, so we let the whole thing drop.'

'Are you upset about not finding him?'

'In a way. But then, if he wasn't interested enough to keep paying Mum, he's probably not worth finding. It was the lies and the pointlessness of it all I found, and still find, upsetting.'

'Denise is getting married soon, isn't she?'

'Yes, in the summer. Isn't that nice?' Lucy had a job to keep her voice steady.

'She's been going out with Tony for a long time.'

'Yes, soon after we left school. He's a lovely man and I'm sure they'll be happy.'

That's more than can be said for Peter or me, she thought. But he'll soon find someone else. With his charm and background he'll soon be snapped up. But her heart cried out that she didn't want him snapped up.

'Have you heard from Ted?' her grandmother asked.

'He wrote me a note saying he'd like to hear from me. I rang a couple of times but couldn't get an answer.'

'I rang about two weeks ago. He sounded funny.'

'Funny?'

'Yes, he kept forgetting what he was saying – losing his train of thought.'

Suddenly Lucy experienced a strange sensation. It wasn't a foreboding, more a premonition that her life would never be quite what she expected. She shivered.

'You cold, love? I can turn up the fire.'

'No, I'm all right. Someone walking over my grave as you used to say. I'm going to Ted's tomorrow, then I can be in everyone's good books again.'

*

Lucy could not hide her shock. Ted was thinner than ever, his eyes like slits in his flushed face. His shirt collar was dirty and the rest of his clothes unkempt.

'What have you done to yourself?' Lucy cried. 'Are you ill? Why have you lost so much weight?'

She surveyed the living room. It had always had shabby furniture that even Catherine had not persuaded him to change. But the room was more than shabby, it was downright filthy and the air was hung with stale smoke and another smell she couldn't identify. 'Doesn't Mrs Gates come anymore?'

'No, she was over seventy. It was too much for her.'

'Couldn't you get someone else?'

'I haven't tried.'

'I thought I'd take you out for a meal. It's the least I can do after neglecting you so.'

'I'll get my coat.' He spoke like a very young child, unquestioning, accepting.

Ted made no comment on her car, nor asked what she had been doing. He seemed unable to communicate voluntarily. He replied to her questions in the simplest manner.

'How's school?' she asked as they drove to a local pub.

'I'm on sick leave.'

Lucy took her eyes off the road. 'Since when? I didn't know. I thought you said you weren't ill?'

'Did I? I'm not ill. The Head thought I needed a rest as I wasn't coping.'

'You haven't got over her, have you?'

'I miss her so, Lucy. She was my life, I just wanted to be near her – now I have nothing.'

She was about to say *you have me* but thought it hypocritical in the circumstances.

'What do you do with yourself all day?'

'Nothing.'

'Don't you read? You were always reading. You and I spent hours at the library and in bookshops.'

'I can't concentrate.'

At the restaurant Ted picked at his food, barely listening to what she was saying. He did ask if she was still going out with Peter, but never mentioned her father. When they returned Lucy said she'd make some coffee. She found the kitchen even more disgusting than the other room. Piles of cups, dishes and glasses, all unwashed, covered every surface. Lucy now realised what the vague smell was.

'Ted, you're drinking, aren't you?'

He took the mug from her. 'Only the occasional one. It stops me thinking.'

'But it's not doing you any good. It's not making you forget, it's making you neglect yourself. You can't go on like this.'

'Why don't you mind your own business,' he yelled, startling her. 'Dispensing largess like Lady Bountiful. Just because you're now some high-class executive, you don't have to come round here telling me what I ought to do.'

Ted had never, ever spoken to her like that, not even when she had done something naughty when she was little. 'You asked me round here,' she said, trying to hold back her tears. 'I want to help you.'

'Everyone wants to help me. Marcie, next door kept bringing me meals till I told her to piss off.'

Lucy didn't know what to say. She was shocked; shocked at his appearance and even more shocked at his state of mind.

'Do you see Richard?' she ventured.

'He and Sheila called.'

'Called? Did you tell them to piss off too?'

'Probably. I can't remember.'

'Can I do anything for you? Would you like to stay with me for a while? A change of scenery might do you good and I can keep an eye on you.'

'Go away and leave me alone. Being in Catherine's flat would be worse than living here.'

It's not Catherine's flat,' she shouted. 'It's mine, I live there.'

She grabbed his still full mug and put it on the tray beside hers and took it into the kitchen.

'I'm going now,' she said on her return. She picked up her coat and put it on. 'What are you doing for Christmas?'

'Dunno.' His brow creased. 'Richard asked me, I think?'

Relieved, she did not pursue his uncertainty. 'I'll ring you. Take care of yourself.' She let herself out.

*

'Where's Lucy?' Peter demanded.

Surprised Emily said, 'Swindon, at Gasson's.'

'Oh yes. Yes, of course.'

'She was going up last night and coming back this evening.'

'I'd forgotten.' He went behind his desk.

'How are you feeling? Did you have a good rest over the weekend? You look better than you did last week.' Emily's expression was concerned.

'Yes, I'm much better, thank you.'

Peter picked up a folder and sorted through the sheets. He had no idea what he was looking for or even which company's folder he had. He snapped it shut, making Emily jump.

'Can I help you? You look mystified.'

'No, I'm all right, but I'm still having difficulty getting back into the swing of things.'

'I can always stop after work and help you if you like.' She looked at him hopefully.

'That's very kind of you, Emily. I can't seem to get going. I'll see how I go.'

*

Peter sat in his car outside Lucy's flat. Not quite outside, that would be expecting too much, but close enough to see when she arrived. He was prepared to stay all night if need be. After an hour Lucy drove slowly past. Five minutes later she walked towards him and turned into her porch. Peter zapped the car and ran towards her, calling her name. The expression on her face left him in no doubt he was the last person she wanted to see. She put the key in the lock.

'May I come in?'

Lucy left the front door open and he followed her upstairs. In the flat she went straight to her bedroom and Peter stood in the doorway watching as she dropped her bag on the floor, unbuttoned her coat and threw it on the bed.

'What do you want, Peter? I'm knackered and all I want is a bath, something to eat and bed.'

'I want to talk to you, get things straight. I...'

Wearily she put her hand to her head. 'There's nothing to talk about. I've told you...'

'Look, you have a bath and I'll cook you something.'

Lucy managed to appear relieved and annoyed at the same time, as she said, 'Oh, very well.'

Twenty minutes later she came into the kitchen wearing a thin housecoat over her pyjamas, her head swathed in a white towel.

'Thank you,' she said primly, as a cheese and mushroom omelette was put before her.

'Shall I cut you some bread? She nodded. 'You look better.'

'Cleaner, if nothing else.'

'Did you have a bad day?'

'Business-wise?'

'Any-wise.'

'I had a lousy journey. Gasson's were male chauvinist pigs and the journey back was worse than the journey up – and the car's parked a busride away. Will that do for starters?'

Peter watched as she hungrily devoured the meal he'd prepared. He knew she was deliberately avoiding his gaze. After what seemed an eternity, he said, 'I saw Stephanie on Saturday.'

'You didn't waste much time,' she said without raising her head. 'Wasn't she the pick of your harem?'

'It wasn't like that. I bumped into her.'

'How convenient.' She pushed her cleared plate to one side and fetched jam, which she slapped on the remaining bread.

'She told me why you won't marry me?'

'Mystic Meg into the bargain.'

'Lucy, listen to me. Please. I told her how much I loved you and wanted to marry you, and did she know why you wouldn't and she said...' He swallowed. 'She said I wasn't the marrying kind and I wouldn't be faithful.' He waited for her response. 'Well?'

'What do you want me to say?'

Peter thought she looked like a little girl as she munched her bread, a jewel of red jam at the corner of her mouth. He wanted to cuddle her. 'Is it true?'

'Only you know if it's true. I can only say what I think – so here it is. She's right. You're not the marrying kind. I didn't want to spell it out because I didn't want to cause you more pain and you're still not fully fit. I tried to stop you proposing in the first place, if you remember.'

'But you're wrong, you're wrong. I've sowed my wild oats. I want to settle down and have lots of coppery-haired children just like you. Don't you want that too?'

Peter came round the table, reached for her hands and pulled her up. She would not look at him. 'Let's go in the other room,' he said.

Lucy let herself be led, and when they were settled on the settee, Peter put his arm round her. He could feel the tension in her shoulders as she shrugged him off.

'Relax.'

'What's this – the softening-up process? I suppose you discussed that with her too.'

'No I didn't. I left her flat and said I would ask you again.'

'Her flat! You mean you were actually in her flat! I thought you said you bumped into her.'

'I did. We had a meal and then I went back to her place.'

Peter realised he'd dug himself a hole he would have a job to get out of.

'See what I mean? You could've said goodbye at the restaurant but no, you couldn't resist going to her flat, could you? You're never going to change.'

'I am. I have. Doesn't it show how I've changed that I did leave? You could find someone you love better than me after we marry.'

'I wouldn't do that, but if I did, I'd be true to any vows I made. All my life people have deceived me – people I've trusted and looked up to. I've had enough of deceit and it's because I love you I couldn't bear it if you went back to your old ways.'

'I'd never deceive you, really I wouldn't. I want to look after you. Goodness knows you need looking after.'

'What do you mean by that?'

'I keep thinking of you that first time we met. You were so childlike.'

'Childish more like. I cringe every time I think about it.'

'So, what do you say? Will you marry me?'

Lucy turned and looked him in the eye for the first time since he'd arrived. Her housecoat fell away and she quickly pulled it into place.

'I've already told you – no.'

'I do love you.' He caressed the back of her neck. 'I'll always love you. Forever.'

'Forever is a very long time, you'd get fed up with domesticity.'

'I wouldn't, I wouldn't. Please say you'll marry me.'

'You're browbeating me again.'

'I promise I won't.' Dramatically he sank to his knees at her feet and grasped her hands. 'Please.'

Weakening she said. 'I suppose everything is in the lap of the gods.'

Peter sensed victory. 'So you will say yes?'

'Well…' Lucy smiled. 'Don't you always get what you want?'

Peter leapt up and gave her a kiss that seemed to last for minutes. The towel fell from her head and he put his hands in her damp hair.

'When shall we get married?' he said, at last.

'Give me a chance. I'd made up my mind not to marry you. Now I find you're setting the date. Slow down.'

'I can't wait, Lucy. You've made me so happy. Just imagine it, living in my house – sorry, our house, and you can change it how you want, and we'll see to the garden together and...'

'Yes, Peter, anything you say, but I really am deadbeat. Do you want to stay the night?'

'In your bed?'

'No.'

'You're very cruel. In that case I'll go home.'

*

Lucy had been working for an hour catching up on neglected correspondence, when Emily put her head round the door and asked if she could speak to her on a personal matter. Lucy was surprised. They got on well, but had never been close. Emily was the daughter of a retired doctor and lived at home with her parents. She had come to the firm straight from college and had worked for David and Peter's father for six years before Peter joined.

'Come and sit down, Emily. We don't often get a chance to talk together, do we?' Lucy smiled.

'I don't quite know how to put this – what to say. You're close to Peter and know him well.'

'I think I've learned a lot about him since I've been here, but you must know him as well as I do - if not better.'

'We've never been what you'd call familiar.' Emily shifted in her chair. 'You will take what I say in confidence. You must never tell anyone else. Promise?'

Emily, reserved and the embodiment of efficiency, was pink with embarrassment. What was she going to say?

'It's Peter.'

'Has he upset you?'

'Oh, no, nothing like that.' She dismissed this as if Peter were the most perfect boss a secretary could have, even though she bore the brunt of his moods and he relied on her to get him out of trouble mostly of his own making. 'It's – it's – I'm in love with him.'

With superhuman control Lucy kept her face neutral.

Obviously Emily was as adept at keeping her emotions to herself as she was. 'Does Peter know how you feel?'

'Good gracious me, no. I wouldn't say – it wouldn't be right. But I'm finding it hard to do my work. I can't sleep, I'm off my food and I can't stop thinking about him all the time.'

'I don't know what advice I can give. If you make your feelings known, you risk a rebuff.'

'I wouldn't say anything. I think the only solution is for me to leave.'

'Peter and David would find you very hard to replace and I would miss you. Are you sure you can't continue?'

'If it gets unbearable, I shall resign.'

What could she say? She could hardly encourage her one way or the other. 'I don't think I've been much help to you,' Lucy said.

'Oh, you have. I had to tell someone. Someone like you who would understand.'

She certainly understood. 'Look, Emily, don't hesitate to come and talk to me whenever you want. Nothing you say or have said will be passed to anyone else. Don't do anything yet. You're needed here, especially as we are expanding. To have someone new to train would be catastrophic. And if you care about Peter, you'll at least see him through this difficult period.'

This must be what blackmail feels like, Lucy thought. She went on. 'But I do understand, because I remember when I was particularly down and had no one to talk to, it made me feel alone in the world. Couldn't you perhaps confide in your mother?'

'My parents are elderly and rather old-fashioned, they wouldn't understand. You seem so wise I feel I can talk to you. You give the impression of being much older.'

Lucy now felt like a fifty-year-old blackmailer.

'I hope I haven't wasted your time,' Emily said. 'You must be busy catching up after taking on Peter's work while he was away. He looks much better this week, doesn't he?' She pushed her chair back and smiled at Lucy. 'I'd better get back to work. I don't want to upset him.'

*

Holding Peter's hand, Lucy skipped along the pavement like a child. The lights and Christmas decorations had taken on a brightness and intensity she had never noticed before.

'Look, look, come and see this.' She pulled him to a toy shop window and watched fascinated as a train wove itself in and out of tunnels and cuttings in snow-covered scenery. 'Isn't it lovely?'

Peter smiled indulgently. 'I've never seen you like this. Every few months you change into someone else.'

'What a bargain you've got.' She reached up and kissed him.

'We're supposed to be looking for an engagement ring, not toys,' he said.

'You could buy a train set now ready for all these children you're expecting me to produce. Then you could play with it.'

'It sounds to me that it's you who wants to play.'

'No, right now I want a ring.'

It was eight before they got back home to Dulwich.

'Your cheeks are quite pink.' Peter took her face between his hands and kissed the tip of her nose. 'And cold. Do you want to go out and eat?'

'No, I want to stay in, snuggled up in front of the fire, while you bring me one of your fantastic meals.'

'Your wish is my command, madam.'

Lucy stretched lazily on the settee. She put her hands above her head, closed her eyes and arched her back. This is what heaven must be like, she thought.

'Wake up, your ladyship. Dinner is served.'

'Have I been asleep? I didn't realise.' She gazed round the room. 'Where is it?'

'Come with me.' He took her hand and led her to the dining room where everything had been laid out for a romantic dinner. Candlelight reflected on the polished table, the glasses gleamed and the light from a small table lamp nearby spread a glow over the room. Lucy's eyes shone and she was speechless. Peter pulled out her chair, shook out the damask napkin and spread it across her lap.

'Oh, Peter,' was all she could say. When he sat down opposite her she said, 'This must be the happiest day of my life.'

'So far,' he replied. 'Think what lies ahead.'

Later, when they were having coffee, Lucy said, 'Would you let me wear my ring – just for a little while?'

'I don't think that's allowed.'

'Please,' she wheedled.

He produced the box from his jacket and slipped the ring on her finger. Regally she twisted her hand to catch the light on the emerald and diamonds.

'We will be happy, won't we, Peter?'

'Without any doubt, my darling. That's what I want and I...'

'…always get what I want,' they chorused.

*

Lucy arrived at Ted's house unannounced next morning. Peter was disappointed she wasn't staying the whole weekend but, as she pointed out, she wanted to do something about the state of Ted's house before he caught food poisoning or some other infection, and she couldn't tackle it when she was tired of an evening. Ted let her in with a faint glimmer of pleasure at seeing her.

'I've come to sort you out. Don't tell me to push off because I shan't take any notice.' She handed Ted her coat. 'I'll start upstairs.'

Before any protest could be made, she was up the stairs and in the bedrooms. By lunchtime she had finished the top floor. Bedlinen was changed, the airing cupboard was sorted and she had put Ted in charge of the washing machine. She didn't stop for a drink and was not offered one. Conversation was minimal. It was now one o'clock and Lucy was tired and hungry.

'Have you got anything to eat in the house? A snack of some sort?'

'I don't think so, look for yourself.'

All Lucy managed to find was stale bread, butter, some biscuits and several out of date tins, which she put in the dustbin.

'Right, go down to Patel's and get these. I've written a list.'

Obediently Ted put on his coat and left.

'I see you're still drinking,' Lucy said, as they sat eating sandwiches. 'Can't you try and cut it down?'

'I don't really want to. What's the point?'

'The point is you've got to get back to work. You won't have enough to live on. They won't go on paying you forever. What do you get now, full pay for so many weeks, then half?'

'Something like that.' Ted jumped up. 'I could do with a drink.'

'No, sit down and listen to me. You were – are – the light of my life, the one person who made things bearable. You cared about me, educated me and gave me a kinder less bitter outlook on life. I wouldn't have done half the things I have if it weren't for you. I love you and it breaks my heart to see you in this state. Not only that, but I think what a loss you are to teaching.'

'Lorraine said that.'

'Lorraine?'

'Yeah, the girl who caused me so much grief.'

Lucy couldn't see how this girl could have said that on the one hand and nearly lost him his job on the other, but she held on to the connection. 'There you are then, everyone knows how good you are. Can't you think about your future pupils? You love teaching...'

'I'm no good at it any more, I've lost my enthusiasm. Things aren't the same.'

'Crap. What you've lost is incentive. Catherine's gone, so you've given up. Can you imagine what she would say if she were here now?'

'If only she were?'

Lucy could see she was getting nowhere and feared she might have gone too far already. 'Well, think about it. Now go for a walk across the Common. That'll get you from under my feel while I tackle downstairs. When you come in you can have a bath and we'll go out. I've put clean clothes on your bed.'

*

'Did you get anywhere with Ted yesterday?' Peter asked.

'I don't think so, not on his drinking. I did manage to clean up his place. Now I've come to work for a rest.'

Peter said, 'I want to talk over Christmas arrangements. My mother rang yesterday and said she was going to my aunt's for the holiday. I couldn't very well tell her she couldn't go because we're going to get engaged, so I just said OK.'

'Ted's been asked to Richard and Sheila's and Nana said she was going to her friend's, so what's going to happen about our engagement.'

'Can't wait to get that ring on your finger again, eh?'

Emily came into Lucy's office saying there was a call for Peter.

'New Year then,' he said, giving Lucy a wink she hoped Emily hadn't seen.

But Christmas did not go as planned and neither did the New Year.

CHAPTER 14

'Who would have thought our great engagement plans would have ended with us having Christmas lunch alone?' Peter said, as they stacked the dishwasher.

'Nice though, wasn't it? Did you think I did everything all right? I've never cooked a whole Christmas dinner before. We were always at Ted's and he did most of the work.'

'I prepared the vegetables,' he said proudly.

'You're a marvel. Quite the greatest thing since the invention of the wheel.'

'Don't get cheeky.'

When they had cleared up they set off to walk down their food. They had eaten early so there were hardly any people around. As they peered surreptitiously into windows, they could see that most people were just about to dine.

'Do you realise,' Lucy said, hanging on to Peter's arm with both hands. 'I shall have my own name when we are married.'

'What do you mean?'

'Well, if my father's name was Evans, and quite honestly I very much doubt if that were the case, then I should be Lucy Evans and not Daniels.'

'Very profound. Now, tell me what improvements you want when you're lady of the house?'

'I love it just as it is. Let me wear myself into it first.'

As Peter put the key in the door on their return, they heard the phone ringing.

'It's for you?' He handed her the phone.

Puzzled Lucy took it from him. 'Hello.'

'It's Richard, Lucy. Ted's in hospital, he collapsed this morning. We're still here.'

'What's wrong exactly?' she asked, but already knew.

'The doctor hasn't made a detailed examination yet, but – but, you know he's been drinking?'

'Yes?'

'He thinks it's to do with that. Ted said to ring you and gave me this number. I tried before but there was no answer.'

'We've just come in from a walk. I think I'd better come over. Which hospital are you at?'

Lucy saw Richard and Sheila as soon as they came into the waiting area at Casualty. They were sitting near the Christmas tree in the corner. An automated sign flashed saying the waiting time was three hours.

Lucy ran over to them. 'Anything happened?' she asked anxiously.

'No. We think they're going to admit him and they're waiting for a bed.'

Sheila said, 'I don't know what's going to happen to Ted. He's in a bad way. We tried to help, didn't we, Richard?'

'I know,' she replied. 'He's not very co-operative.'

Lucy thought that if she'd not been so wrapped up in her own affairs she could have prevented all this.

'I don't know how he'll cope when they discharge him,' Sheila said, echoing Lucy's thoughts.

A doctor approached. 'I'm the casualty consultant', he said. 'Who am I speaking to?' His eyes took in the four of them.

'We – my wife and I – brought him in. We're his friends and he's staying with us over Christmas.'

'I'm his – his stepdaughter,' Lucy said.

'I see. Well, your stepfather is suffering from acute pancreatitis, but we need to do a scan. I gather he's been drinking heavily.'

They all nodded.

'I must warn you that if he goes on doing so his condition will become chronic and eventually kill him.'

Lucy stared at her feet. She recalled all the bottles she had found poked away in various places, as well as in boxes under the sink. She realised that she had kidded herself his drinking had been moderate and that he could stop if he put his mind to it.

'What you are saying is that he's an alcoholic?' It was the first time that Peter had spoken since they'd arrived. Lucy had almost forgotten he was there.

'Yes,' the consultant confirmed.

'What's going to happen now?' Lucy asked.

'The abdominal pains and vomiting will probably last for forty-eight hours. We'll keep him in for at least that time, depending on the scan. Then he'll be discharged.'

'But he lives on his own,' Sheila exclaimed

The doctor shrugged his shoulders. 'You can go and see him now, but he will still be in pain till the analgesics take effect.' As he turned to leave he said, 'There are pamphlets on alcoholism at reception.'

'I'm going to get a coffee,' Peter said. 'Anyone else want one?'

'This has rather spoiled your Christmas' Lucy said to Sheila. 'Would you like to see Ted first, then you can go home and rescue your lunch.'

'We hadn't got as far as cooking the turkey,' Richard said. 'You will keep us posted, won't you?'

'Of course.' She swallowed and her brain fast-forwarded to the problems that she could foresee.

When they had left she looked for Peter who appeared, holding two plastic beakers.

'I brought you this. Where are the others?'

'Gone to see Ted, then I said I'd go.' She took a sip of the liquid and turned up her nose.

'Not much cop, is it?' Peter said. 'You're not going to stay long, are you? I hate hospitals.'

Ten minutes later Richard and Sheila said their goodbyes, their faces showing their concern.

'Oh, Ted,' was all Lucy could say when she stood by his bed, before bursting into tears.

'Don't cry, Princess. I'll be all right after a few days the doctor said.'

'Only if you stop drinking. Please don't drink any more, you'll kill yourself.'

'I'm OK, I just have to take it easy, that's all. Don't worry.'

'But I do.'

'Did you have a good Christmas? I think I've spoilt Sheila's.'

Before she could answer, he doubled up in pain and a nurse came over as he was about to be sick. When he had been cleaned up, he lay back on the pillows his breathing laboured, his forehead wet with sweat.

'Is – is Peter - with you.'

'Yes, he's outside. He doesn't like hospitals.'

Ted smiled wanly. 'I'm not - too keen - myself.'

'When you get out you will give up, won't you? Just for me?'

Lucy kissed him and brushed away her tears as she left.

She was quiet on the way back to Dulwich, turning over in her mind what she could do. She flopped into the armchair and putting two fingers over her lips tried to get her mind round the day's events.

'Did you hear what the doctor said, about Ted probably coming out in two days. He can't look after himself and he'll start drinking again. I really didn't think it was as bad as this. What shall I do? Will it be all right if I take some time off?'

Peter frowned. She knew he wouldn't be pleased, which just added to her anxiety.

'I can work from Ted's place if you get me fitted up with a computer. And I can come to the factory on some days. Nana will help me.'

'I'm not very happy about this, Lucy. A few days aren't going to see him better, not even a few months from the sound of it.'

'I've got to do something!' she cried, distraught. 'I can't just leave him to drink himself to death. Is that what you're suggesting?'

'Of course not. Don't be so melodramatic. I just want you to realise that this is not flu, or some bug like I had, that's going to go away.'

'What do you suggest if you're so far-seeing?'

'Let's not argue, we're both done-in. We can discuss it in the morning.'

*

Lucy got her grandmother's co-operation and Mrs Daniels was at Ted's house when she brought him home. He refused to stay at Lucy's flat.

'How are you feeling?' Nana asked.

'Bloody awful, if you must know. I could do with a drink.' He went into the living room and rooted round the sideboard. 'Where's the whisky I left in here.'

'I threw it away,' Lucy said. 'You know what the doctor said and you promised me.'

'I didn't promise you anything and I don't care what the doctors say, I'm going out to get some.' Ted headed towards the door but Lucy put out a restraining arm.

'Please don't. Let's try to work something out between us. I can't help you unless you help yourself.'

'I don't want your help. If I drink myself to death that's my lookout.'

'But it isn't, it's mine as well. You told me you would try to stop. Don't you realise how much you're upsetting me? Can't you think about me like you used to – your Princess?'

Something in her tone, or maybe the word Princess, stopped him. He returned to the living room and sat scowling in his chair. Lucy went into the kitchen and she heard her grandmother hesitatingly ask if he was in pain, to which he replied only for want of a drink.

'Do try to do what Lucy says, Ted. She thinks such a lot of you and she's awfully upset. She was crying when she phoned me after she came back from the hospital.'

Ted sat morosely letting the words flow over him till Lucy came back and handed her grandmother a mug of tea.

'Now we must have some plan of campaign. Nana and I are going to take it in turns to stay here. I know how you feel,' Lucy said, seeing the expression on Ted's face, 'but I can be as determined as you can, if I put my mind to it. I know it's not going to be easy, not for any of us, but if we all try we can get somewhere.'

Lucy was anxious to establish her position, to convince him. Ted pulled a face but managed a slight lift to the corner of his mouth that Lucy hoped was a smile.

'I'm going to find out the local branch of Alcoholics Anonymous.'

'I'm not an alcoholic,' he protested. 'I can stop if I want to, I just don't want to.'

'But you are and you must face that before we can do anything.'

'Can't I have a tiny drink,' he wheedled, 'a sherry or something.' His eyes pleaded with her and she felt such a love for him.

'Think back to when I was younger.' she appealed to him. 'The coaching you gave me, the school holidays we spent visiting museums or going to plays. Oh, so much I can't think of it all. Doesn't it mean anything to you that you can't let me return you to good health?'

'Of course it does, Princess, I'll try. Now what about that small drink.'

Lucy let out a long breath. She knew she shouldn't give in, that he should never have another one, but at the moment she had to get some organisation into his life. She gave him a small sherry, at the same time investigating exactly what bottles there were in the house and how she could dispose of them when he wasn't looking.

Lucy only took one day off from the factory. A plan was devised whereby Mrs Daniels would be with Ted during the day and Lucy would relieve her straight after work and live at Ted's for the time being. Peter put up as many objections as he could, but Lucy was adamant.

'I'll be with you at weekends, including this one – New Year. We can still announce our engagement.'

'I don't think that's a good idea.'

'Not a good idea? Why not?'

'You're in the middle of something you think is going to be over in a few weeks. I don't want our engagement squeezed into other events as if it is of no importance.'

'If I'd known, I'd have asked Ted to put off being ill for another month.'

'Pity he didn't.'

'All right, have it your way. Do you still want to see me Friday night to see in the New Year?'

'Of course, we'll just celebrate it quietly together.'

'Yes, yes, we'll do that.'

Lucy couldn't understand why she felt so uneasy about putting off the engagement. After all, it was only for – but Peter hadn't said for how long.

*

The situation was working out better than expected, Lucy thought as she let herself into the house one Thursday night three weeks later. She went into the living room and was pleased to see that Ted was reading a book. He shut it with a snap as she came over.

'How've you been today?'

Nana said, 'He went for a walk while I did a few chores, didn't you Ted?'

'Yes.'

'Did you ring up about AA?'

'Sorry, I forgot. I'll do it tomorrow. Promise.'

When their meal was finished and Lucy had seen her grandmother off, she returned to the living room. They usually watched television together or read. Ted wasn't there. Frightened, Lucy went into the hall and called, 'Ted, are you all right?'

'Yes. I'll be down in a minute.'

'Right, I'm here now,' he said as he crossed the room to sit in his usual chair. 'What's on the box?'

Lucy peered round the room for the *Radio Times*, which she saw beside Ted's chair. Reaching across to pick it up she smelled the whisky on his breath.

'You've been drinking!' She glared at him. 'Where did you get it? When you went for your walk, wasn't it? I thought you seemed a bit high when I came in. How could you?'

'Don't be angry, I am trying. This is the first since I came home from hospital.'

'No it isn't. What about the sherry you've had of an evening and during the day judging by the bottle.'

'I don't count that.'

'Alcohol is alcohol. You've got to stop!'

Ted reached for her hand. 'Don't get upset. You're such a lovely girl. So like Catherine.'

'I'm nothing like my mother and she certainly wasn't lovely. The only thing we had in common was red hair. I'll tell you one thing, if she were here now, she'd be much harder on you than I am.'

'I know.' He smiled at her. 'Come and sit on my lap like you used to.'

'Oh really Ted, don't you think I'm a little past that?'

Nevertheless, she did, and was immediately thrown back to her childhood; to the hours he spent with her reading books far in advance of her age. Often she did not understand, but Ted seemed to know when that was and would explain or ask questions to find out the level of her understanding. Lucy was never bored. She loved the stories and the sound of Ted's voice. Even now, when she noticed the children home for the holidays, her heart gave a lift of contentment recalled.

'Do you remember reading 'I, *Claudius*' with me, and all those questions I asked about the sexy bits which I couldn't understand.' Lucy giggled. 'I couldn't think why you were so tongue-tied. I had to ask Denise, who was always the fount of all wisdom to me, especially where boys were concerned. I don't think she was sure – we were only about twelve.'

Ted was quiet, staring into space.

'Where's the bottle, Ted?' Lucy asked softly.

'In my bedroom.'

*

Lucy let herself into the house and was grabbed as she went to close it.

'Peter,' she gasped. He released her slightly, but continued kissing her face. 'I've heard of a warm welcome, but this is ridiculous.'

'How can kissing you be ridiculous?' he whispered in her ear.

'All right, startling.'

'It's hell not seeing you all week.' He put up his hand, 'and don't tell me I see you every day.'

'It's not the same, is it?' Lucy agreed. 'When we meet at the factory I want to rush up and kiss you. Have you said anything to David? He keeps giving me funny looks.'

'No, but when I was ill, I did tell him I was going to ask you to marry me.'

'What's for dinner?'

'I'm afraid I've taken the easy way out and bought prepared food, but it won't take long in the microwave. Fancy a drink?' As he went to the sideboard he asked, 'How's Ted?'

'Still drinking. He went for a walk Thursday and bought a bottle. He'd drunk two- thirds before I found out.'

'What did you do?'

'I threw the rest away, but I can't stop him buying more. We talked about old times when he used to read to me, hoping he'd focus on how things were before, but it all gets linked to my mother and he keeps saying how much I'm like her.'

'Are you?'

'Only our hair. She was tall and beautiful with hazel eyes. I'm short and fat with blue eyes. Facially, I don't think we resembled each other at all. But red hair is quite a statement and we probably have some of the same mannerisms, so I suppose I do remind him of her.'

'You're lovely Lucy – and I've told you before you're not fat, that is what I've seen. Now, if you'd let me see more of you, I could give a better considered opinion.'

'We could go swimming, you'd see more of me then.'

'You are heartless, sadistic, merciless, unfeeling…'

'…caring, warm-hearted and extremely loveable,' she finished.

'I'll going along with that,' he said, putting a drink in her hand.

Lucy dismissed Ted from her mind for the rest of the weekend. While Peter read the paper, Lucy wandered round the house studying each room deciding which bedroom could be a nursery for the children Peter was hoping for. From what her mother had said, after one she would never want any more. Catherine was fond of telling her what a terrible time she had had when Lucy was born, but Nana told her it was an easy birth.

Together she and Peter viewed the garden which, as its future owner, Lucy saw in a new light. Neither of them had any knowledge of gardening, so they thought of the fun they would have discovering the names of plants already there and perhaps redesigning it altogether.

'My mother did all the gardening. What's here now is the result of more than thirty years' hard work. She's always nagging me to get a gardener. I only cut the grass when I think about it.' He gave a rueful smile. 'Talking about my mother reminds me, I must put those photos back in the loft.'

After dinner Peter fetched the cardboard box from the dining room. On the landing he undid the trap door and pulled down the ladder.

'Look, I'll go halfway up and you can hand me the box. It's not too heavy, is it?'

'No, it's OK.'

Lucy picked it up and raised it above her head with one hand. The box wobbled. She put up her other hand to steady it, but too late. It tipped to one side and the photos scattered all over her head, on to the landing and down through the banisters to the hall below.

'Are you all right, darling?'

Lucy laughed. 'I'm fine – just clumsy.'

Peter came down the ladder. 'You sure?' he said, picking a photo from the top of her head.

'I thought I was balancing it so well. I'll go downstairs and pick up the ones in the hall and you do these.'

She ran down the stairs and started gathering them up. Lucy called up to him. 'I'm afraid a lot of them have come out of their pockets.'

'Can't be helped. I don't suppose my mother will ever look at them again.'

'This is a good one of you,' she called. 'Your hair was shorter and curlier. If you have it that short again, do you think it'll grow curly?'

'Not very likely. It began to lose its curl when I was thirteen or so, and when I left school I let it grow longer. Do you want me to have it shorter?'

There was no reply. Peter looked over the banister. Lucy was sitting back on her heels, in one hand was an envelope, in the other a photograph.

'Lucy? Lucy, what's wrong?'

She raised her head, eyes glistening, and then she lowered it.

'No, oh Peter, no. Not that.' Slowly her head moved from side to side and tears dropped on the photo in her hand.

'What is it? Are you all right? Did you hurt yourself after all?'

He rushed down the stairs two at a time and knelt beside her. He took the photo from her hand and laid it on the floor with the others.'

'Look at it Peter. Look at it!' Her voice cracked.

He glanced down. 'It's my father, so what? What's wrong?'

'Do you see who's with him?'

He peered at it again. 'No, I can't say I do. Someone at a business do he went to, I expect.'

'It's my mother.'

CHAPTER 15

The enormity of the situation overwhelmed them.

Peter said. 'It can't be. No. How would they have met?' Then, 'Are you sure?'

'I do know what my mother looked like,' she spat out, more distressed than she could have imagined possible. Lucy stared at the photograph again. Peter's father in a smart suit, her mother in a full-skirted dress and, in the blurred background, other couples. It was obviously taken at some dance hall by a professional photographer. Lucy recalled her grandmother's words *your mother would go anywhere to dance.*

'You do realise what this means?' Lucy studied his face as her words sank in. 'He must be my father.'

Devastated and angry, Lucy paced up and down the hall. 'Wasn't I the fool searching for a Peter Evans. She lied about everything else, why not about his name – but it was only half a lie – just enough to get me searching, as she knew I might one day. How could she be so vindictive? She must have suspected who you were all along.'

Lucy ran up the stairs. Peter found her sobbing, face down on her bed.

'I can't bear it. What have I done that my life should be ruined every step I take?' Her voice was muffled in the duvet. 'I was so happy – so happy.'

Peter sat on the bed stroking her hair trying to think of something to say – but no words would come. There were no words to reassure her. There was nothing that would be of comfort to either of them.

Far into the night they talked, trying to sort out the implications. Should they tell anyone? If so, who? Her grandmother? David? Everyone? Announcing it as if they were coming out? What effect would it have, especially on Peter's mother? They even tried to convince themselves that it was not what they thought, but Lucy knew it was.

Could they see each other every day feeling as they did, knowing what they knew? Should they sever all contact, exchanging cards at Christmas like distant relatives, as indeed they were? Questions, problems, but no answers, no solutions.

Lucy said. 'I'm tired, I don't want to be alone tonight. Can I sleep with you? I need to feel you close.'

'But…' he began.

'No buts, this is between you and me. Whatever we decide, I want part of you to take into the future. A reminder of what might have been.'

*

Peter walked to a pub he hadn't been in since he and his friends had drunk there as under-age teenagers. The walk down the hill was meant to clear his mind, but it had done nothing of the sort. He took his beer into a corner and opened the part of *The Observer* he had grabbed as he left the house.

They had not made love. He had slipped into bed beside Lucy who was half-turned from him. He curved himself round her and put his arm across her waist. With his other hand he wove his fingers into the hair at the nape of her neck.

'I love you Peter,' she said. 'Hold me tight.'

How could one have such a passionate desire to make love combined with an equally strong reluctance? He knew that if she made the first move, he would not be able to resist.

When Lucy said she wanted to sleep with him he wasn't sure that it was literally what she meant. He still did not know. She had always been so adamant that she would not do so. His charm had always worked on other women, but never on Lucy. In a perverse way he had found this endearing. He had lain very still, the length of his body curled about hers until he heard her deep even breathing and knew she was no longer awake. When he was sure he would not disturb her, he rolled on his back and stared at the patch of light from a street lamp shining through a gap in the curtains. His illness had brought Lucy close to him – how ironic.

Peter had risen early after a restless night and slipped out of bed, leaving Lucy asleep. While getting coffee, Peter thought about his father. He couldn't imagine him with another woman. To him, his parents always seemed happy and he had never been aware of any tension. True his mother wasn't an outwardly demonstrative person, but his childhood had been a contented one. Perhaps his mother's miscarriages had caused a rift. The liaison with Lucy's mother would have been about that time he calculated.

Lucy said money had been sent for some years, then stopped. Why had it stopped? He thought his father an honourable man in that respect. Had his mother found out? Could it have been about the same time the firm was in difficulties? Perhaps David would know, but neither of them had come to any conclusion regarding who, if anyone, should be told.

Peter took a sip from his glass and opened the newspaper.

Lucy had left after breakfast saying she wanted go back to Ted's. Jealously he thought she might discuss the situation with him and he didn't want her to. They had tried to talk about everyday things but between them was a culpability they could not come to terms with. Lucy had cried heartrendingly as they kissed goodbye.

Peter felt out of control. He'd always been confident, doing what he wanted, when he wanted. Even returning after his father's death had not been an unwelcome summons. He was always ready for a challenge. But the wretchedness facing him now was unbearable. His dream of settling down with someone he truly loved was just that – a dream.

Peter drained his glass and left the pub, leaving his unread paper on the table.

*

Lucy went to the flat first, then drove from Clapham to Streatham. She thought about the previous night. It was her intention that Peter made love to her. He had been so warm and comforting as he lay beside her that she had closed her eyes and knew no more till morning when she woke alone and bereft. How she wished they had made love. Who worried about convention? Who would care? Who knew about their relationship anyway?

When she arrived at Ted's she told her surprised grandmother she would take over. Ted overheard and said he resented being regarded as a prisoner in his own home and why didn't they both shove off. Mrs Daniels was close to tears, but Lucy had hardened her heart.

'Don't take any notice of him, it's the drink – or lack of it at the moment. Has he kept off it?'

'I think so, but he's been very bad-tempered. I've tried to keep out of his way. It's terrible to see him go downhill so. I am very fond of him.'

'Let's go out for a walk,' Lucy suggested when her

grandmother had gone. 'It's cold but quite sunny. It'll do you good.'

As soon as the last sentence left her lips she regretted it. Ted went on about interfering women who wanted to do him good, and swore in a manner that Lucy had never heard him use in her presence. She did her best to ignore him and, putting on her coat and handing him his, he finally gave in.

'Why don't you ask me what I've done this weekend,' she asked, not that she intended telling him of her appalling situation.

'I'm not interested.'

'You were once. I used to pour my heart out to you. I told you all my secrets – well, nearly all.' She squeezed his arm and smiled up at him.

'Well, I'm not now. Anyway, you've got Peter to tell your secrets to. I'm irrelevant in your life.'

Hurt, she said, 'You'll never be irrelevant in my life, that's never been true and it still isn't. I love you, you know I do.'

A small dog came yapping at their legs and Ted struck out at it with his foot. 'Get off,' he shouted.

The elderly owner glared at him and called the dog away.

'What do you think of Peter?'

'Don't know enough about him to give an opinion. You rarely talk about him.'

'Not much point if you're not interested.'

The sun was low and bright. She took her hands from her pockets to shade her eyes. 'Its colder than I thought. You all right? Want to go back now?'

'What I want is a drink?'

'The pubs won't be open it's Sunday afternoon.'

'There must be some pub round here that's open all day.'

'I don't know of one. I don't know much about pubs at all.'

Ted tramped morosely beside her.

'Did you ring AA?'

'Oh, for God's sake shut up. No I didn't and I shan't go anyway. I can stop drinking if I want to,'

'Very well, let's go back. Can you get the fire going like you used to? I do miss an open fire.'

'Chimney's not been swept,' he snapped.

*

Peter brought his coffee into Lucy's office during the morning. As blue looked into blue, kin to kin, their wretchedness was reflected.

'When I left my flat I nearly came back to you yesterday. I wanted to hear you say you loved me,' Lucy told him.

'Why didn't you?'

'I thought it would only make me more depressed when I had to leave. I can't believe life can be so vengeful. Ever since I was born I've been thwarted. My mother wouldn't let me do this or that for no apparent reason, other than spite. I try to get away but that doesn't work out and now I've reached the most joyous period of my life and what do I find? She's even reached from the grave to deal her ultimate blow.' She stirred her coffee and tears ran down her face. 'On top of all that, there's Ted.'

'Don't cry, Lucy. Perhaps we can work something out.'

Lucy did not hear what he said. 'It was only as I got older that I realised how much she hated me. When you're a child you accept as normal treatment what you later realise is not right. I was a constant reminder of how she'd been let down.'

Peter turned his face away.

'I'm sorry, I still cannot take in he was your father too.'

'But Ted loved her to the point of lunacy according to you.'

'Unbelievable, isn't it? She didn't treat him much better than she treated me, though he did occasionally turn on her if she pushed him too far. I suppose she was good in bed and that was enough for him.'

'Good enough for my father too, it would seem,' Peter said, picking up his cup and saucer and moving towards the door.

'Does it hurt you very much to know he was unfaithful to your mother – albeit for only a few months?'

'Yes, it does. I like to think my parents' marriage was perfect.'

'You didn't mind spreading your light around from what you've told me.'

'But I never went out with married women – not to my knowledge.'

'My mother must have known your father was married and had a son. She wasn't bothered about breaking up their marriage.'

'She might not have known and she was very young,' Peter said kindly.

'I don't see that as an excuse, hateful woman. Talk about *"for the sins of your fathers"*. If anyone is *"undeservedly atoning"* it's us.'

'Is that a quotation? You are clever.'

'Not doing me much good, is it?'

'Look, next weekend we'll really thrash this out and come to a decision.'

*

Peter sat in the armchair with Lucy at his feet. He removed the pins from her hair so it fell to her shoulders.

'Ted used to do that to Catherine.'

'I love your hair. I was hoping that our…' His voice tailed off and she felt his fingers tighten, unaware he was hurting her.

'So, what decision have you come to?' she asked. 'Shall we tell anyone what we've discovered?'

Peter was quiet for a long time. 'I don't know how to live without you,' he said.

'But we can't leave things as they are,' she insisted.

'You seem so strong, Lucy.'

A strangled sound came from her. 'If you only knew. I'm forcing myself because one of us has to.' She got up and sat bedside him. He put his arm round her and pulled her close. 'Let's study each option logically,' she said.

'Love isn't logical.'

'This has to be. We can't get married.'

'But if we hadn't found that photograph, we would be getting married.'

'But we did and we do know. I suppose we could still marry, but we couldn't have children. I wouldn't like that and neither would you.'

'We could adopt,' he suggested.

'You're not thinking this through. You would want your own child to carry on the family name. You'd look at me one day and see a sister, and at someone else's children and know they weren't yours. I know you Peter, you wouldn't be able to do that.'

'So – we can't marry. What other suggestions have you?'

'Tell everyone what we've discovered, I'll resign and leave the area.'

'I don't want my mother to know.'

'I'll just resign then – make some excuse. It'll cause a stir for a while, but everyone will soon forget.'

'I won't.'

'You're being negative. We must reach some conclusion.'

Lucy was trying to be resolute, but each solution she put forward only seemed to make the hurt deeper. The thought of never seeing Peter again was intolerable.

'David's going to ask me the outcome of my proposal any

minute. What'll I tell him?'

'Tell him I refused.'

'Where does that leave us?'

There was a pause while Lucy regarded him thoughtfully. Then she said it, just as she'd told Peter he couldn't be faithful. 'I could live with you.'

'Lucy!'

'You're shocked?'

'I can't help it. You sound – you sound more like me. I wouldn't dare to have suggested such a thing.'

'I'm acting more like your Stephanie.'

'I don't think of you like that,' he said forcefully. 'I love you. I've told many girls I've loved them when what I meant was I liked making love to them. It's not the same thing. I've never fallen in love before.'

'Poor darling.' She hugged him.

'Anyway, I don't want to sully your name,' he said.

'That sounds quaint,' Lucy said. 'But it'll be your name being sullied.'

Peter's mouth widened into a smile of such charm she thought her heart would break. 'Is that what you really want, Lucy?'

'Given the circumstances, yes.'

It seemed so neat, all tied up like that in a package, but Lucy knew it was only a short-term solution. When the time came for them to part, as indeed it must, there would be even more sorrow and anguish. By then they would have known the joy of their love and companionship. For now she would live for the moment. Didn't she deserve some happiness, however transitory?

*

From that momentous weekend and the weeks that followed, Lucy managed to cope with Ted of an evening, deal with her work during the day and make love to distraction at weekends.

'You're the sexiest woman I have ever known,' Peter said one night.

'I find that hard to believe,' she said as she snuggled closer, 'though I must admit I would never have thought of doing what I've done, or where I've done it.' She giggled.

'Lucy, I do love you.'

They would fall asleep in each other's arms forcefully driving to the back of their minds the knowledge of the price they would eventually have to pay.

Eleanor stood at the window of her flat. She looked out to the common that sloped away to the centre of the town and surveyed the tall spires that jutted up into the sky and the rocky outcrops with houses nestling close. She speculated on who, in the past, had enough clout to build on a common.

She felt lonely and uneasy. She often felt lonely and realised it had been a mistake to leave the family home quite so soon after Jack died. She ought to have stayed longer, maybe a year or so till she'd adjusted. She had hoped Peter would soon marry, and having a future mother-in-law in situ might put off some young women.

Wholeheartedly Peter had thrown himself into the business when she'd asked him, and she thought he hadn't indulged in his favourite womanising past time. He had assured her he had never brought any women to the house since she'd left, apart from Lucy.

Eleanor watched a car draw out from the line that parked along Mount Ephraim. How long would that space remain free, she wondered. But no sooner was the thought out of her mind than the vacant bay was occupied. She turned from the window with a sigh.

They had all been down yesterday to discuss the business. Eleanor thought it was kind of them to come to her, but she was getting less and less interested, even though she was a large shareholder. Figures and forecasts had been discussed but she'd switched off and studied each of them.

David had aged since she'd last seen him. What was he now – sixty-six? Should have retired and been at home enjoying the grandchildren. Wonder how Bridget is? Never took to the woman. They'd only formed a foursome for business socialising.

Peter was brimming with good health. She had never seen her son look so contented and he could barely take his eyes off Lucy. Though she didn't gaze at Peter with the same adoration, her face was animated. There was a glow to her usually pale cheeks and her blue eyes shone like pale sapphires. There was something about her that Eleanor could not quite define. Self-satisfaction? No, that made her sound smug. Intelligent and efficient she undoubtedly was, as her son never ceased to remind her. And the way she looked after Peter when he was ill had Lucy almost endangering her own health. When the business was over and Peter and Lucy had left, she tackled David.

'What are those two up to?'

'I've no idea. He as good as told me he was going to ask Lucy to marry him, since then – nothing.'

'Could it have something to do with her stepfather – Ted, isn't it?'

'Could do. It must put a strain on her. Maybe they're waiting till he's better to announce the day.'

'She seems very fond of Peter.'

'Do you fancy her as a daughter-in-law?'

'More than any of his other women, not that I saw any. Peter knew my views.'

'I don't think he ever saw them as prospective wives.'

Eleanor grunted her disapproval. 'Thank goodness for that.'

'You know you asked me if he and Lucy were sleeping together?'

'Yes.'

'Well, she once told me she wouldn't.'

'Is that so, well, well, well.' Lucy rose higher in her estimation.

Eleanor moved to the kitchen. There was something else troubling her. It was there when she first met Lucy. She reminded her of someone. Was it a person she'd known in the past or a celebrity that she'd seen on television? It was so annoying that her mind would not function as she wanted. The names wouldn't come, the relevant words escaped her. Old age she supposed. She made herself tea and took it back to the drawing room.

*

The call came at the office about four on the Wednesday before Easter.

'It's no good Lucy, I can't stand it a minute longer.' Her grandmother was crying. 'He says the most dreadful things – and he's drunk most of the time – and he's – he's breaking things up. I don't want to stay here any more. I've d-done my b-best.'

Lucy could hear noises in the background. 'I know you have, Nana, don't upset yourself. I'll come right now, just wait till I get there. Go out in the garden out of Ted's way. I'll be with you in half an hour.'

When she arrived Ted was slumped in his chair in a drunken stupor. He barely acknowledged her. The carpet was littered with fruit and broken ornaments which he'd swept from the sideboard. Lucy went to find her grandmother.

'I'm sorry, Lucy love, but I can't stay here. I've tried to persevere, but I haven't told you half the things that go on 'cause I didn't want to worry you. But I've come to the end of my tether. You'll just have to make other arrangements.'

'OK, I understand. I didn't realise you'd put up with so much. He seems calmer in the evenings when I get here. I suppose you've been bearing the brunt of his worst moments.' Lucy put her arm round her grandmother. 'I'll take you home. I need to call in my flat for the mail. It seems as if he has drunk himself to sleep, so he'll be all right till I get back.'

Lucy's flat was cold and unfriendly. She hardly stayed there now and her great idea to refurnish had come to nothing.

The post collected and the newspapers disposed of, she glanced round to see everything was safe and returned to Ted's.

'Your Peter rang, said would you ring him at home.'

'Thanks.' Lucy began clearing the floor.

'Leave that where it is. I'll do it later.'

'I'll do it, the fruit might get trodden in the carpet.'

She ignored his disgruntled mumbling and continued what she was doing. She knew he was in no fit state to argue. In fact, she was beginning to understand all his varying moods, from the maudlin to the frustrating and frightening. She went to her bedroom and rang Peter on her mobile.

'But what about going away this weekend?' he wailed when she explained the situation. 'It's all arranged. I was looking forward to it.'

'I know, but I can't leave him.'

'But what about me?' His voice took on the petulant tone she used to find so irritating when he couldn't get his own way.

'There'll be other weekends.'

'It's not the same. We were going to get married this spring – remember?'

'That flew out of the window long ago.'

'But I want to be with you as often as possible. You keep telling me we must enjoy each other while we can.'

'Come over here then. I know it's not so good, but we'll be together.'

'I don't want to come over there. I want you here with me.'

Softly she said, 'I could do with your support' and clicked off the phone.

Peter arrived about seven.

'Would you like to come out and eat with us?' Lucy asked Ted.

'No I wouldn't.'

'Shall I get in fish and chips then?'

'Do what you like, I probably won't eat them.'

Peter said, 'Lucy's only trying to help. Couldn't you at least meet her halfway?'

Lucy wished he'd keep quiet.

'What's it got to do with you? I didn't ask her or her grandmother to come round poking their noses into my business.' He stared at the empty glass on the table beside him. 'I want a drink.'

'You'll kill yourself.'

'So what? Who cares?'

Peter went to speak again, but Lucy threw him a warning look before saying, 'I care. I care very much. Please try to beat this then you can get back to teaching.'

Suddenly Ted burst into tears. 'I'm no good any more. I used to take such interest in the children, wanting them to do their best, trying to give them a love of literature and language and – and…'

Lucy rushed over and hugged him. 'You will again, honestly, together we can beat it. We can do things together like we used to, go to plays and things, concerts, galleries. Think of all the school holidays we spent going round London. It was so wonderful. You don't realise what pleasure it gave me. We could do that again, couldn't we? Just the two of us. I could take time off, couldn't I, Peter?'

But Peter had left the room.

*

'You can't go on like this Lucy?' Peter said a few weeks later.

'I'm all right. Ted's so much better now and we did manage to get away for part of the Easter weekend, thanks to Richard and Sheila.'

'But you're looking so tired and you've lost weight. The strain is showing.'

'I'm all right I tell you. He'd not been drinking for three weeks now.'

'That's what you think. As soon as you come back to work I bet he resorts to the bottles he has hidden.'

'Oh, stop nagging. You're worse than Ted.'

'Has he nagged you?' He was concerned.

'He gets a bit belligerent at times. It must be difficult for him because there are no half measures - literally. He must stop completely, not even a small glass of sherry.'

'I wish you would leave him to get on by himself. It's not your problem. We were so happy together. Can't we get back to how it was before? I miss you so much.'

'I know you do darling, and I miss you too, but I want to see this through.'

'It could take years.'

'I don't think it'll be that long. You're being pessimistic.'

Lucy knew she was deluding herself. She had read about alcoholism at the library. But even she didn't realise just how many demands would be put upon her.

*

Negotiations with other factories saw a crèche get underway with great success. Mothers from all over the site would stop and tell her how grateful they were and why couldn't something like that have been done before. Their gratitude brought a little relief to her life. Most of her days were assuming proportions she was finding it difficult to deal with. She would wake up in the morning thinking about Peter and their love for each other then remember her duty to Ted.

Eventually, Lucy badgered a reluctant Ted to Alcoholics Anonymous. He said it would be a waste of time as he wasn't an alcoholic. He didn't go every week, but someone from the group would fetch him if he missed a session. He would drink in spurts, sometimes going several days without a drink. As Peter surmised, Lucy would find empty bottles in the dustbin and others secreted in various places, even though Ted emphatically denied he had touched a drop.

But Lucy realised that the moment she and Peter had been putting off now had to be face.

CHAPTER 16

'Come in, Denise. It's lovely to see you. How are the wedding arrangements going?'

'Everything seems under control, though no doubt some hitch will crop up nearer the time. Now, what's this great decision you want to tell me about? You sounded rather mysterious on the phone.'

'You know I'm living at Ted's most of the time?'

'Yes, your grandmother told me when I saw her the other day. I gather he's going through a bad time?'

'You could say that. He's been drinking heavily on and off, mostly on, ever since Catherine died. I was so wrapped up in my own affairs I didn't spot what was going on. If I had I could have nipped it in the bud. I feel so guilty about him, that's why I'm living there.'

'I really don't think you can blame yourself – after all, he isn't even a relative.'

'I know, but he was as good as. Look what he did for me, I'd be in a psychiatric ward if it wasn't for him.'

'That's as may be, but gratitude is not quite the same as guilt. He's the one who chose to drink.'

Lucy took in what she was saying, but Denise could not understand what a debt she owed Ted, even if he hadn't turn to drink.

'How long are you intending to live at Ted's and carry on with your job. You're looking peaky as it is.'

'That's why I've asked you here. I'm going to resign.'

'But you can't do that,' Denise said alarmed. 'What does Peter say?'

'I haven't told him.'

'Hasn't he asked you to marry him yet?'

Lucy hesitated. How much should she tell her? Only she and Peter knew their secret; better keep it that way. 'Yes, but I refused.'

Denise threw up her arms. 'I don't understand you at all.

After nearly twenty years you're still a mystery to me. You're telling me that you're giving up an exceptionally good job in a firm owned by a man who wishes to marry you, who'll give you a life of comparative luxury – and you've turned him down? Is there something I'm not being told here?'

Lucy wished Denise weren't quite so intuitive. 'I want to be with Ted and I can't do both.'

'I'm sorry, but I don't believe you.'

'Let's take our coffee into the other room,' Lucy said. 'You can tell me how your plans are going.'

'You don't shake me off that easily. You may love Ted and owe him your undying gratitude, but no one gives up what you've been offered – not after what life has dealt you in the past.' She moved over to Lucy's chair and put an arm around her. 'It's something serious that's come up. Is it Peter? I did warn you. Isn't he the man you thought he was?'

'You could say that,' Lucy said, close to tears. She reached for a handkerchief. 'I don't want to go into details. I would, if I could, because you have been such a good friend to me and I've always confided in you. But this is something I must keep to myself.'

'Must? That's a funny word to use. You're not in any trouble are you? You sure I can't help?'

'I'm sure. I just wanted to put you in the picture – well, half a frame.' Lucy gave her friend a weak smile.

'He hasn't hit you or anything, has he?'

'Good heavens, no. He loves me.' She said this more vehemently than she intended for it made her decision even more bizarre.

'I suppose you know what you're doing,' Denise said. 'But it all seems very strange to me.'

One down, two to go.

*

Lucy went to David. 'I want to give in my notice,' she said, coming straight to the point.

She waited for David to make his protestations, but he beamed at her and said, 'Peter doesn't want you to work after you're married. You'll be difficult to replace.'

It was Lucy's turn to be taken aback. 'We're not getting married. I'm going to take care of Ted and I can't work here in such a demanding job. I might have to take something in an office that doesn't need much thought – copy typing or something like that.'

David was stunned. 'With a brain like yours – what a waste! What's Peter done that's upset you? He intimated ages ago he was going to marry you. His mother and I have been waiting for some announcement. It's obvious he's dotty about you. You might think you've been hiding your feelings, but everyone knows how you two feel about each other.'

'Oh dear, do they really? We thought we were being so careful.'

'You make a better job if it, but Peter can't. What you see is what you get with him. Come on, tell me what's really troubling you. You know I want to retire soon. Two of us going would put a great strain on the company.'

Lucy explained as she had to Denise, but he didn't believe her either.

'There's more to this than meets the eye. Has he ill-treated you or do you think he might? He does have a quick temper.'

'He'd never do anything like that, you know he wouldn't.'

David was still frowning at her, then said, 'You doubt he'll be faithful to you?'

Admitting this would let her off the hook, but she chose to say nothing.

'Does Peter know you're leaving?'

'No, and I don't want you to mention it to him. A month is all I need to give, isn't it?'

'Yes,' David said reluctantly. He picked up a file and put it down again. 'I can't tell you how upset I am about this. You're a great asset to us and will be hard to replace. And on a personal note, I shall miss you very much.'

'No one is indispensable,' she said, her eyes filling.

'But some are more dispensable than others.'

When she left David she went along to Emily's office.

'Are you very busy, Emily. I wonder if I could have a quick word.'

Emily turned from her screen her expression cold and dismissive. 'What do you want? I do have rather a lot to do.'

'I wonder if you'd come to my flat after work, or perhaps meet me somewhere. I have something I want to explain to you'

'There's no need to explain if it is what I think it is. Peter's face has said it all.'

'I do need to talk to you. It is very important to me.'

*

'Happy birthday, Princess. I didn't know what to buy you, so I got a book token. You can't go far wrong with that.' He gave her a puzzled look. 'Or did I give you one last year?'

'Yes, but not to worry. We can go to the bookshop together next weekend and you can recommend something. I need a bit of culture, I've hardly read anything for the last couple of years.'

'Won't you be at Peter's?'

'No, not next weekend. He has to go away somewhere.' She tucked the token in her handbag. 'We could go for a drive, down to Brighton maybe, what d'you think?'

Ted had been considerably better the last few weeks and Lucy was sure he hadn't been drinking. She hadn't found any evidence though she had searched.

'You're filling out a bit. Do you feel better?'

'Yes, a little. You've been very good to me, especially when I've been so awful. I don't mean it. Well, I suppose I do at the time, but you know I really care about you.'

'Me too, Ted. I can't tell you how pleased I am to see you getting back to your usual self.'

For how long she wondered. He'd had good phases before. Still this one had lasted longer than the others. Could it be the beginning of the end?

'Where are you celebrating tomorrow night?'

'Peter's taking me to a show, like he did last year.'

She thought of last year's attempt at seduction. Poor Peter. Poor Lucy. She hadn't known what she'd been missing. He was certainly some lover. Her throat constricted as she thought of what she must tell him tomorrow night.

Lucy wore the emerald dress and the peal necklace Peter had given her. She left her hair down as Peter preferred. To hide her apprehension she laughed a lot and told him stories about when she was a girl and how shy she was. So shy she wouldn't go into shops and made Denise go in for her. She told Peter about the time they went to buy their first bras. Even Denise had been a bit embarrassed, but with her usual aplomb had marched up to the counter with one for each of them. They had little idea they had the right fit and giggled in Denise's bedroom at this great step into womanhood.

'I bet you were a sweet little girl,' Peter said in the taxi back to Dulwich.

'I don't think so. You ask Denise? I was so uptight most of the time. It's funny how shy people draw attention to themselves by their very shyness. Many's a time I've wanted to crawl into a hole and die. My mother used to go up to a policeman and then tell me that she'd told him what a bad girl I was. I was convinced they all knew about me at the police station. It was years before I realised it wasn't true. Even now I get a strange feeling when I see policemen.'

'How could anyone be so cruel?'

'My mother was very practised.'

'Do you think it was because of what my father did?'

'Partly, but according to Nana, she was always awkward and domineering. I think she led my grandparents a merry dance. Nana was always a bit afraid of her.'

'Poor darling. Never mind, tonight I'm going to love you so you can forget all your troubles.'

If only. The thought of what she was to say to him made her heart heavy. However, when they had made love, her courage failed and she fell asleep in his arms.

Peter heard a noise and strained to hear what it was. He turned towards Lucy. 'What's the matter?' He switched on the bedside light and glanced at the clock. 'Lucy? Lucy, why are you crying?'

She had her back to him but he could hear her sobs muffled in the pillow. He pulled her towards him.

'Aren't you feeling well? What are you crying for?'

'We c-can't go on. The time has come.'

'What are you talking about? Are you having a bad dream?'

'I meant to tell you before we went to sleep, but I couldn't.'

'Tell me what?'

Lucy sat up and reached for a tissue. 'We must end it now. Stop seeing each other. It had to come, you know it did. And I think this is the time.'

Peter did know, but he didn't want to face it, not now, not at this moment. Later, sometime in the future – the distant future.

'You will still see me at the factory.'

'I've given in my notice.'

'What! You never told me.'

'David's in charge of personnel.'

'Stop splitting hairs. You've still to give a month.'

'I gave in my notice a fortnight ago. I only have two weeks to do.' She turned to him. 'Please don't be angry. I don't know how I'll manage. I need you to see me through. We need to see each other through.'

Lucy started crying again and he put his arm round her. 'I can't believe this is happening. Perhaps we could get married,' he said helplessly searching for a way out. 'I don't mind about children it's you I want. Nobody ever need know.'

'We've been through all that. What we're doing now isn't right.'

'Who cares about convention?' he said.

'I do, and in your heart of hearts you do, too.' She paused. 'Don't you?'

He lay back on the pillow. She reached for his hand and they lay like that staring at the ceiling finding no ease in the contemplation of their future.

'What'll you do?' he asked eventually.

'I'm not sure. I haven't discussed it with Ted yet, but I might give up my flat and live at his place permanently.'

'Lucky Ted,' he said bitterly.

Lucy raised herself on one arm and stroked his face. 'You'll find someone else, Peter.'

With a quick movement he turned his face away. 'I don't want to love anyone else. Only you. Only you.'

'Oh, my darling.' Lucy put her arm round his waist and kissed his broad back. 'It had to be.'

*

How she got through the following two weeks Lucy did not know. Because David and Emily knew of her decision, they did their best to be businesslike with the two of them.

As usual, Peter took his feelings out on Emily. Lucy thanked her for what she was doing and reminded her of their conversation. David and Gordon walked around with long faces and, when news of Lucy's leaving reached the factory floor, their faces were glum. Colin said that production had slumped.

'You're kidding,' Lucy said when he told her.

'Well, slowed down a bit. You're going to be badly missed. Who'll stick up for us now? Peter's been a right pain in the neck.'

'Everything will settle down in a few weeks, you'll see,' she reassured him. Except what she was feeling inside.

*

When Ted heard she'd given in her notice he said he hoped it wasn't for his benefit. He wasn't worth that sort of sacrifice and he was well now. Lucy assured him that she did want to look after him, but that was not the only consideration.

'There are complications at work,' she told Ted. 'Peter and I have had a row.'

Lucy didn't elaborate and could not decide when she suggested giving up her flat, whether Ted was pleased or not. He tended to vacillate between gratitude and resentment. She did think she'd detected some relief in his eyes. Still, it was no good having doubts now. The deed was done.

Peter threw a party for her and invited all the staff, including the factory workers over whom he had once been so disparaging. Perhaps she had softened him a little.

As well as a collection many of the girls had bought her small individual gifts like brooches or handkerchiefs. Lucy spent the whole evening wiping tears from her eyes.

David picked her up and brought her to the hotel. Ted had been invited but declined, and Lucy was glad because she thought the available alcohol would have been too much of a temptation.

'I'll drive you home,' Peter said at the end of the evening.

Lucy put the box of presents on the back seat and slipped in beside Peter. Apart from thanking him for the evening, they were silent.

'There's an omen,' he said as a car drew away from the kerb right outside her place. 'That's the closest I've ever been.'

Lucy forced a laugh. 'I've never parked this close.'

Peter turned off the engine and they sat not knowing what to say. He reached into his pocket and pressed something into her hand.

'Here, take this, my darling. My parting gift.'

'Is it my engagement ring?'

'Yes.'

Tears rolled down her cheeks in rivulets, continuous and unchecked. 'I can't, I can't.'

'Please take it. And remember me when you wear it?'

'I'll never forget you, my dear, dearest Peter. You'll always be the love of my life. Be happy.' Lucy squeezed his hand and quickly stepped from the car. Peter picked up the box from the back seat and carried it to the door.

'Shall I take it up for you?'

'No, I'll manage.' If Peter came up to the flat she knew they would only prolong the dark moment.

'One last kiss?'

'One last kiss.'

They clasped each other tightly and their tears mingled.

'I don't know how I'm going to live without you.' Peter said.

'You will, my love. Time will heal.'

Lucy turned and let herself into the hall. As she shut the door she could see Peter's outline through the stained glass as he leaned against the porch wall.

*

It was Saturday, the morning of Denise's wedding. Lucy was to be chief bridesmaid. She stared at her dress of apricot silk hanging on the front of the wardrobe.

Ted was to drop her at Mrs Gannon's house that morning and go on to her grandmother's for a coffee before taking Nana to the church. Judging by last night there was no way he would be fit enough to walk let alone drive. Lucy had begged him to keep sober for twenty-four hours. Couldn't he do that just for her? But the row had taken its usual degenerative course – misunderstanding, self-pity, lost pride.

'Mrs Gannon? I'm sorry to ring you when you must be so busy, but could Nigel, or someone, pick up Nana later. I'm afraid Ted isn't well enough. I'll drive myself over, but I won't have enough time to deal with Nana as well.'

'Of course, my dear. I'm sure we can rustle up someone to fetch her. There seem to be enough people milling around the house.' She laughed, then more seriously asked. 'Are you all right?'

'Yes. Don't tell Denise about Ted. I don't want her upset on her special day. See you later.'

Unshaven and still in his dressing gown, Ted staggered into the living room and headed for the sideboard.

'I've arranged for someone to pick up Nana.'

'Nana? What for?'

'It's Denise's wedding today. When I've had a shower I'm going to the Gannons. I'll leave you something in the fridge for midday. I expect I'll be home to get something this evening. There won't be much point in my staying for long.'

Ted's face clouded over and she saw his eyes fill. Too upset to console him she went up to the bathroom.

*

The weather had been perfect, the speeches were over and the

166

buffet eaten, but mixed with the pleasure of her friend's happiness was Lucy's misery. Peter should be with her as her husband, an old married couple of two months or more.

Lucy sat at one of the tables, her hand clasping a near empty glass of orange juice, which she was swirling round and round. Sylvia and Joe Gannon looked happy as they mingled with their guests. Tony's parents seemed a little shy. She ought to go over and speak to them but she couldn't summon the energy to do so, or move from her little haven in the corner of the large room.

Waitresses were still clearing the tables and music was being relayed from unseen speakers. She drained the last of her juice and a waitress whisked her glass away almost before it touched the table. With nothing to hold Lucy felt more naked and vulnerable.

Should she be helping Denise change? Where was she? Ah, over there, still in her wedding dress and looking so beautiful. How she had always admired her kind, loyal friend. A voice above her made her jump.

'What are you doing here all alone?' It was Tony's best man.

'Hello – um.' What was his name? Her mind was blank.

'Mike.'

Lucy's face burned with embarrassment. She knew his name perfectly well. He perched on a chair beside her.

'Denise tells me you've been going through a bad time. She didn't give me details, so there's no need to think I know your innermost thoughts.'

'I'm not feeling very sociable, which is a dreadful thing to admit when you are the chief bridesmaid. Did Denise send you over?'

'Yes, but it's not a chore.' He gave her a smile that reminded her of Peter – but then everything reminded her of Peter.

'I'll put you in the picture, then you can say what you like without feeling you're treading on eggshells. I've broken up with someone I love very much, gave up my job because I worked for him and I live with my stepfather who's an alcoholic.'

'That'll do for starters.' He gave another smile. 'Denise says she wants you in...' He looked at his watch, '... twenty minutes. That was to be my excuse for coming over. It'll give me enough time to tell you all about myself.'

Lucy couldn't help laughing, he was so likeable.

It did take him about that long to tell her he had met Tony at university, that he was a civil engineer and lived with his mother in

Tadworth in Surrey. His father had left his mother when he was ten and he had no girlfriend at the moment. Lucy wondered if his was an opening she was meant to pursue. But she wouldn't be company for someone as lively as he was. She would bore him to tears and someone sparkling and vivacious would come on the scene and she would be told he'd felt sorry for her.

'You look very pretty.'

'Did Denise tell you to day that as well?'

'No,' he said indignantly, 'I'm quite capable of doing my own complimenting.'

Lucy studied his features. Fair hair, long thin face slightly flushed – too much champagne. He was taller than Tony she'd noticed in the church which would make him six foot plus. She glanced up and saw Denise signalling.

'I'll have to go now, duty calls. Thank you for the chat.' Lucy stood up and Mike caught her hand.

'Could I give you a ring sometime?'

Lucy hesitated. Mike would bring some relief to her drab life. No. No matter how hard it was going to be Ted was her priority.

'I'd rather you didn't. I'm not in a position to – to -, but thank you all the same.'

'How did you get on with Mike?' Denise's muffled voice queried as Lucy eased the cream, silk dress over her head.

'He was very charming, told me his life history and asked if he could ring me some time.'

'I hope you said yes?'

'No.'

'But why? You're making yourself a martyr. Ted's drinking could go on for years, for the rest of your days even. You must make a life of your own.'

'I've told you, I wouldn't have a life at all if it hadn't been for Ted,' Lucy said, straightening the folds of the dress and putting it on a hanger.

'You can still keep an eye on Ted and have some fun surely.'

'Go from man to man, you mean, till they find out there's no future with an alcoholic in tow. I don't think so.'

'I still think you're making a big mistake. I like Ted, you know I do, but I really don't understand what's behind what you're doing. He chose to wallow in self-pity after your mother's death. It wasn't as if he'd been a heavy drinker and her death had tipped him over the brink.'

Denise zipped up her skirt and reached for the matching blue jacket.

'How long before you and Tony leave?' Lucy wanted to know when she could decently slip away.

'We're going about half seven, eight. We want to join in some of the dancing after the band has arrived.' She moved to the mirror and combed her hair. 'My parents have done me proud, don't you think?'

'I wish it were my wedding. I miss Peter so much.'

'If he's so keen and you love him so much, why on earth don't you marry him. You said he wouldn't make a good husband, but look what you've taken on in its place, infinitely worse. If you were already married you wouldn't have considered living at Ted's then, would you?'

'I know, I know,' she cried. 'It's so complicated.'

'I don't understand,' Denise said hopelessly.

'You go and find Tony and I'll change out of my dress and be with you in a moment. Off you go.' She gave Denise a hug and pushed her towards the door. 'You looked so lovely today, and still do.'

*

Dreading what she would find, Lucy let herself into the house. Ted was in his chair asleep, a bottle and glass beside him. The air was thick with alcohol fumes. She opened the window wide.

'How did it go?' he asked, barely opening his eyes.

'Denise looked gorgeous. Everything went well and Nana seemed to be enjoying herself. When I left she was dancing with Denise's father.'

'I'm glad.'

'Have you eaten?'

'I had one of the sandwiches you left.'

'Nothing since?'

Ted shook his head.

'Would you like a take-away, Chinese, pizza, fish and chips? I don't feel like cooking.'

'Whatever you like, I don't mind.'

'Couldn't you make one small decision other than how much you're going to drink,' she snapped.

'Pizza then.'

*

In the following months Lucy greeted most mornings more tired than the previous evening, if that were possible. She would climb into bed and lie clutching a pillow pretending it was Peter before drifting into a restless night. Then would come the unwelcome morning with Lucy wondering what demon would be inhabiting the body of her almost unrecognisable Ted.

In the New Year she had a welcome call.

'Hello, Lucy, it's Denise. Happy New Year.'

'And to you. How are you both?'

'Soon to be three.'

'Oh, how wonderful. I'm so pleased.'

'We're off to America soon. Tony has been offered a job in Boston and we're going to see the lie of the land. When we come back, we'd like you to be the baby's godmother.'

Peter and I could be expecting a child by now, the first in a long line of redheaded children.

'Hello, Lucy? You there?'

'Yes, sorry. I'd love to be the baby's godmother. I'm honoured you asked me.'

'How are things with you? How's Ted?'

'Much the same – still drinking.'

It was very quiet at the other end. 'I'd better ring off now,' Denise said. 'I'll let you know the date.'

'Don't forget to tell me when the baby arrives first.'

'Of course I won't. Bye Lucy.'

'You'll miss her,' Ted said when she relayed her news.

'It's funny, I don't see much of her, but I always know she's there. A bit like a guardian angel.'

'Still, there's always the telephone,' Ted said.

Lucy was about to say ringing America would be a drain on finances, but this would be seen as a reproach - as indeed it was.

*

Lucy was bowed down with depression. It required a supreme effort on her part to keep up any semblance of interest in her job or the home. Her office work was tedious and gave her no satisfaction, other than the money. She would come home, cook a meal and spend the rest of the evening slumped in front of the television. Concentration or making any simple decision was almost impossible. The days stretched ahead endlessly with no sign of a let-up in tension. Denise's words rang in her ears. Ted could go on drinking for the rest of your days. So much for thinking she would cure him if she gave him the tender loving care she thought was all he needed.

Was she sacrificing her life for some misplaced loyalty she owed Ted? She had not been exaggerating when she said Ted had saved her sanity. He was there to stick up for her when she needed him, someone she could turn to who knew and understood the misery her mother put her through. But how much of what Ted had done for her was she meant to repay? Or was compassion, like love, a commodity that had no boundaries.

'Ted,' she called, 'lunch is ready.'

Lucy put the bowl of soup and bread on the table beside his chair and went back for her own. As she returned with a tray she called upstairs again. What on earth was he doing now? He had gone up to wash and shave after breakfast, come down for his usual whisky and told her not to bother getting him a coffee. She had not seen him since because she had been in the garden all morning sweeping up leaves and generally tidying up. Lucy put a plate over her soup and went upstairs.

She found him lying on his back with his hand clutching his stomach.

'Ted, Ted, what's up? How long have you been lying there? Are you in pain? Can you get up on the bed?'

There was a groan and he took a sharp intake of breath. Lucy grabbed her mobile and rang for an ambulance.

At the hospital she saw the same consultant she'd seen eighteen months before.

'Well, Miss Daniels, he has already damaged his liver and probably other organs. If he doesn't stop immediately he will be in constant pain till he dies, in the not too distant future I must tell you.'

'How - how long, if he doesn't stop now?'

The consultant shrugged. 'Months.'

'And if he does stop?'

'Hard to say, a year, maybe two.'

Ted stared at Lucy as she stood by his bedside, his appearance that of a man in his late fifties.

'I'm dying, aren't I?'

'Oh, Ted. Why have you done this to me?' Tears rolled down her face and she pushed a handkerchief into her eyes to stem the flow.

'I'm sorry, Princess.' Ted reached out his thin hand and Lucy took it in both hers.

Unchecked the tears coursed down her cheeks. 'Please stop, please. Do it for me, your special Princess.'

'I'll try.' He smiled weakly and screwed up his eyes as another pain struck him and he vomited into a bowl on the bed.

She kissed his forehead and left, unwilling and too emotional to stay longer.

When she returned home she rang Ted's mentor. Frank was a reformed alcoholic who had been assigned to Ted at one of the meetings. He would pick him up and try to encourage him to go if he was reluctant. Not that he often succeeded. Frank said he would come round and see her before going to the hospital.

'You know, Lucy, there isn't anything that can be done by either of us if Ted doesn't want to do it. Until he admits his problem to himself, he'll go on drinking. I hope you won't mind me saying this, but I think you do too much for him – you're always there as his prop.'

'But I try, or rather I tried, to make him see the consequences of what he's doing. It isn't as if he's a horrible person. He's wonderful, kind and clever. What more can I do? Do we live together till I bury him? I love him, Frank. No one could have done more for me within the strange circumstances we lived under.' Lucy thought of her father and his heartless indifference to her and her mother.

'Unfortunately, it's not in your hands, is it? Having said that, if and when he comes home, you will have to be cruel to be kind. Then we'll see what he's made of.'

When Ted came out of hospital he told Lucy he was going to give up drinking. When he saw her sigh, he said, 'This time I really mean it Lucy. The doctor said – he gave me only six months if I don't.'

'I know, Ted, but it's up to you. You do realise, don't you, it might already be too late?'

Two weeks later Ted came back from his solicitors. 'You will not want for anything when I've gone, Princess.'

In bed that night Lucy thought of her future without Peter and soon without Ted. Would they sit watching television together till her dear Ted died in pain before her eyes? What sort of life would she have then?

CHAPTER 17

'They're here, they're here,' Lucy shouted from the back door before rushing to the front. She flew down the path as Denise emerged from the car. Joyously they hugged each other.

'Oh, it's so good to see you, Denise.' Lucy looked into the car. 'And my darling Gemma. Haven't you grown, but you won't remember me.'

Denise lifted her daughter out of her seat and set her on the pavement. Lucy went to take Gemma's hand, but it was swiftly put behind her back. 'You were a tiny baby when I last saw you, just like your little brother is now.'

'I'm nearly frwee.'

'I know – very grown up.'

Tony released the baby seat and came to join the two friends who were leaping up and down with excitement.

'This is Christopher, six months old last week.' Denise proudly showed off her son.

Ted came round the side of the house holding the hand of a toddler who could just about walk. He shook hands with Tony and kissed Denise.

'Don't let's stand out here,' Ted said, lifting up the little boy. 'Come on in. I'll just wash my hands. I've been doing some gardening, helped by my trusty assistant.'

'I can see that,' Lucy said, taking in the muddy clothes. 'Better wash him too.'

'That's Jimmy, I presume. How old is he?'

'Sixteen months. Ellie is in her pram. I'll fetch her.'

'Ellie? You haven't got another one? You are a dark horse. How old is she?'

'Two months.'

Lucy made coffee and they talked about Tony's job in Boston, how much they liked it there and couldn't wait to get back.

'Nana wrote that Nigel has married. She saw your mother last week.'

'Yes, nice girl.'

Ted joined them. 'We tried to persuade Lucy's grandmother to live down here near us, but she said she was a Londoner through and through and wouldn't know what to do in the country.'

'It took us some time to settle,' Lucy said. 'It seemed so quiet after London, but Somerset suits us fine and the fresher air down here will be good for the children.'

After lunch the men were told to take Gemma and Jimmy for a walk while the babies were having their afternoon naps so Lucy and Denise could have a good natter.

'I've had so much to ask you,' Denise said when they'd gone. 'You didn't answer any of my letters and if my mother came across your grandmother, she was always so cagey. What were you trying to do, disappear off the face of the earth?'

'I know, I'm sorry, but my life was – well, I didn't have much of a life to tell the truth. I used to get so depressed and found it hard to make any decision, even what to wear next day.' Lucy laughed. 'It's unbelievable, isn't it? The last time Ted was taken to hospital he finally realised he'd soon be dead. One of his AA friends said I was doing too much for him. So I ceased getting meals unless I was eating with him. I no longer washed his clothes or cleaned up after him. I did the minimum of housework.' She laughed. 'That wasn't difficult because I never felt like it. I made myself go out several evenings a week – that was an effort I can tell you. One day, Ted told me he had tipped all the drink he had in the house down the sink.'

'So he hadn't stopped after he left hospital like he said.'

'Yes, he had, but Ted had bottles hidden all over the house, so it was a very positive move he made.'

'Was it as simple as that?'

''Fraid not. Even though he'd given up drinking, he had terrible bouts of depression, because of the withdrawal of alcohol. These were difficult for me and him to cope with. But I still made him look after himself. One day I saw him going through his bank statements and though he thought I hadn't noticed, I could see how shocked he was at the dip in his savings.'

'This is fascinating,' her friend said.

'Fascinating isn't quite the word I'd use.'

'Sorry, it must have been awful for you, but it sounds like something from a film where you are waiting for the next scene.'

'I'll keep you in suspense then and get us some tea.'

Ten minutes later they had settled down once more.

'Ted had been off the drink for several months so I thought I would ease up and not go out so often. I'd wash his clothes but not iron them. I ordered the *Times Education Supplement,* an extravagance at that time, I can tell you. I would read out the odd article but make no comment. Ted started going to the library and went back to reading his poetry books. I still kept up the disinterested act waiting and hoping for him to make a move.'

'Then what happened?'

'It was quite miraculous. One day he said to me "This sounds interesting" and read out a teaching job that had caught his eye. My heart was pounding but I tried to keep cool. I said why didn't he search for other posts he thought he could do.

'There were times when the fear of not being able to cope would throw him into despair but he didn't resort to the bottle. Then I really stuck my neck out and suggested we get married.'

'What a shock that was when I heard. What did Ted say?'

'What you'd expect – that he was twenty years older, that I was like his daughter and it wouldn't be right. I said that the age difference didn't matter – lots of men were that much older than their wives – and who cared anyway. Then he argued it would be more difficult to walk away from him if we were married and that he would be a burden.

'We argued, he found excuses, but I wore him down. I finally persuaded him and – glutton for punishment that I am – suggested he sells the house and move out of London. We kept looking in the TES until we found the post he has now.

'Suddenly we were married, moved and he was teaching again. It was a terrible time in one way because he was taking several very big and stressful steps. We both were. He hadn't had a drink for a year and there was a chance that all the upheaval might be too much.'

'Ted has aged terribly. His hair is almost white.'

'I know, it's taken its toll. It's a bit embarrassing when he's taken for Jimmy's grandfather, but it doesn't bother me and Ted is so besotted with the children he's not worried either.'

'Is he over it now.'

'You're always an alcoholic, Denise. We just take each day as it comes. His health is not good; his drinking did him a great deal of harm. Ted won't live …Trying to prevent her tears, she went on, 'He's already past the doctors' forecasts and is now on borrowed time. Having Jimmy has given him a focus. He dotes on that boy. Do you know he reads poetry to him after he's read a bedtime story? And the other day I saw him leaning over Ellie's cot saying *"Shall I compare thee to a summer's day".'*

'If nothing else they'll be well read,' Denise said. 'How did he take to teaching after so long a break?'

'He found it very hard. But I used to help him with the preparation and marking to begin with. He wasn't given an exam class but any teaching is very demanding and things had changed since he last taught.'

'The school were taking a big risk, weren't they?'

'Yes, but he was honest with them. The Head at St Jude's gave him an excellent reference which went down well and he was on half a term's probation.'

Denise studied her fingernails. 'Does Ted – you know?'

Lucy frowned. 'Does he what?'

'Mention your mother when, um … Forget it, I'm being too personal.'

Lucy giggled at her embarrassment. 'Does he think of Catherine when he's making love to me – is that what you're asking? I've really no idea. We rarely talk about my mother and even then in the most general terms. To be honest, I don't give a toss.'

Lucy took the tray into the kitchen. When she returned Denise asked, 'What happened to Peter? Do you know?'

Lucy stared out of the window. 'He married last year.'

'Is this going to take long?' Emily had asked, when she arrived at Lucy's flat. She wore the same frosty expression she had in the office earlier that day.

'Peter has asked me to marry him but I've refused,' Lucy revealed.

'Refused!' Emily exclaimed. 'You've refused, yet he goes around in a state of euphoria. I don't believe you.'

Lucy went on. 'You know, don't you, that I have a sort of stepfather, though he and my mother never married? Since my mother died he has been drinking heavily. My mother neither loved nor cared about me, but Ted did. Had he not come into my life I would have been suicidal. Now he's in trouble and I'm going to give up my job and look after him.'

'Give up your job.' Emily was reeling from Lucy's revelations.

'Peter will be devastated.'

'I know, and that's why I wanted to talk to you.'

'You want me to dry his tears and console him. Well, I can't do that, not for you, not for anyone. I don't know how you can ask that when you know how I feel about him. You were more than a little deceitful when I foolishly confessed this.'

'I'm sorry about that, but I want you to do more than that. I want you to marry him.'

'Marry him! What do you mean?'

'You will have to bide your time, be subtle, let him do all the pursuing without him realising. It'll take some time because we are very much in love. But Ted needs me.'

Emily sat for a long time without speaking. Lucy had difficulty imagining her and Peter together.

'You do understand what I'm asking, don't you, Emily?'

'Your stepfather must be some person.'

'Do you know who he married?' Denise asked.

'Yes, his secretary.'

'Oh, you must have known her. Is she nice?'

'Yes, very. She understands Peter and will know how to manage him.'

'How do you know all this? Are you still in contact with him?'

'No, but he rings Nana now and again. I didn't want him to know where we'd moved to, but I didn't mind if she passed on other news. The latest I heard was that Emily was expecting. David Willman stayed on another year after I left, but has now retired and Peter has been busy because of the new people he's had to train. I think the factory is doing well.'

They heard Tony and Ted at the back door.

'Who'd have thought our lives would have turned out like they have,' Denise said. 'Me in Boston, you in deepest Somerset and two children apiece. You never know what's in store in life, do you?'

'As long as we're happy that's all that matters.'

'Are you happy?' Denise questioned, raising an eyebrow.

'As long as Ted is, I am too.'

'That doesn't quite answer my question.' Denise gave her friend a long, hard look. 'I suppose you still don't want to tell me the full story. It wasn't as straightforward as you made out, was it?'

Tony came in the room carrying Gemma, followed by Ted

with his baby replica. His curly hair fell over his forehead as his father put him down and he toddled two or three steps, then crawled over to his mother. Lucy lifted him on to her lap. He reached out a chubby hand for the biscuits.

'Greedy guts.' Lucy tickled him and stroked his soft, cold skin with the back of her finger. 'You look more like your Daddy every day – and just as hungry.'

'I resent that slur on my character,' Ted said laughing. 'Shall I go and fetch Ellie? I can hear noises from upstairs.'

'I'll come up with you,' Denise said.

'That leaves Tony to play with Gemma and Jimmy while I get the meal.

'Lucky me,' Tony said. 'Where's the toy box?'

*

It was the week before half term when a large envelope addressed in Lucy's grandmother's handwriting arrived as Ted drove off to school. Inside was a letter from her grandmother, a plain envelope marked Lucy and an official-looking one addressed to Mrs Lucy Lassiter.

Nana wrote saying Peter had rung wanting to know her address for an important reason, but she wouldn't give it to him because of what Lucy said. He was not best pleased she could tell, but a few days later he came to see her and said his solicitor wanted the enclosed letter to get to Lucy urgently.

Lucy opened the plain envelope first.

> *My dear Lucy*
>
> *You will be sorry to learn that my mother died a month ago. She had a slight stroke and a week later another more serious one.*
>
> *Before her final stroke we had a long talk. To my surprise she spoke about you all the time. time, how lovely you were, how she had missed you and how much she wished we had married. But, even more amazing, she asked was the reason we didn't marry because we had discovered that Dad was your father too? You can imagine how I felt. I just stared, probably with my mouth open. There wasn't much point in denying it, so I asked what made her suspect. She said there was something about you that had puzzled her from the moment she first met you. And after you'd gone away, it*

suddenly dawned on her one day that when you
were deep in thought or worried, you had a similar
expression to that of my father. The more she
thought about it, the more she recalled some
of the same mannerisms. The fact that we hadn't
married and that you'd left so abruptly seemed to
confirm her suspicions. A few days later she died.

I expect you were surprised to hear Emily
and I married. We had a girl last week and she
suggested we call her Eleanor Lucy because she said
you were always so kind to her. I hope you are pleased.

Your grandmother let slip (she was very loyal
about your instructions) that you now live in Somerset.
I would like it if we could be in touch with one another
again now we have settled down. Emily and I would
love to see you, Ted and the children.

I have never spoken to anyone about what we
discovered and I assume neither have you.

I hope Ted is well. Your grandmother told me
he is now teaching again. I am pleased for
you both.

Peter

The second envelope contained a letter from the firm of
Davell & Co. It informed Lucy of the death of Mrs Eleanor
Margaret Evans on 23 September. It went on to say that in her Will
she had left Lucy Daniels three thousand pounds and half her
shares in Evans & Co. They understood that she had since married
and they would like a copy of her marriage and birth certificates,
after which they would deal with the bequest.

Lucy sat bemused by this latest turn of events. Fancy Peter's
mother noticing a likeness to her husband – her father. It was so
wonderful she couldn't get over it. What did she do when she was
deep in thought? Was she doing it now? What expression did she
have that was like her father's? Why hadn't Peter noticed?

What now? She couldn't show Ted Peter's letter. If she did
tell Ted the truth, he wouldn't believe she married him for his sake.
Why should he think otherwise?

She read her grandmother's letter again. That didn't mention
Peter's note, thank goodness, just that Peter had told her about
Emily having a girl. She could show both letters to Ted tonight.
She screwed up Peter's note and stuffed it in the pocket of her

jeans.